Storm Over South Central

An anthology from the
heart of a man

Written By
Charles L. Chatmon

Adrolite Press
California

Acknowledgments

I give thanks to the Lord Jesus Christ for allowing me to live this far on the journey despite my shortcomings and for blessing me with the words to write so that I may share them once more with you, the reader.

To my wife, Chandra. Every day with you is a blessing, and every day since I've met you has been the best day of my life.

To my mother, Elizabeth, thank you for your love, encouragement, instruction, and support. I am blessed to be the son of two beautiful people. I love you with all my heart.

Much love to the Chatmon and Jenkins families, uncles, aunts, and cousins. Thank you for believing in me and showing support in my writing endeavors. All my younger relatives who dream the same dream as I did years ago never stop reaching for the top. You will make it.

Thank you to my brothers and sisters in Christ. May the Lord be with you always.

To the rest of my friends guess I did it again, huh? Thanks for being by my side through the highs and lows and the good times we always have at the Super Bowl parties.

To all my fellow online and social media friends, thank you for putting up with me. (smile)

To everyone I've met in my role as executive director of the L.A. Black Book Expo. It was a learning experience.

I thank you from the bottom of my heart to everyone I've met along this journey through life. It's my continued hope your journeys will be rewarding as mine. Never, never stop praying and pursuing your dreams from the depths of your souls and the voices of your heart.

Dedications

Mary Jenkins
"Mother"

My father, Charles L. Chatmon, Sr.
I will always miss you Chat. Thank you for being such a great father to me. I love you and always will make you proud of me, no matter what.

My aunts Katherine McClintock, Deloris Ball
and uncle Russell Chatmon, Sr.

And so many others I knew who have moved on, young and old.

I love you all. I hope I made you proud of me.

Your grandson, son, nephew, and friend,
Charles L. Chatmon

ABOUT THE AUTHOR

Charles L. Chatmon is a native of Los Angeles, California. He is a graduate of California State University, Los Angeles and has years of experience in the educational field. He is a contributor for local community newspapers and magazines. Mr. Chatmon is the former executive director of the L.A. Black Book Expo. He taught writers workshops in Los Angeles and the San Francisco Bay area for years.

A Note from the Author:

In light of the changing times in our society and even in our neighborhoods, most of what you read may have no bearing on the area you live in. Therefore, please treat these works as a history lesson, occurrences we who still live in this community grew up with. I believe you will find it a most rewarding experience.

Take care!

Charles L. Chatmon

Contents

Intro: From the Inside Out

The Observer greets you once more.....

I can't walk on waves
or part the Red Sea
just using what
the Creator
placed inside of me
not pursuing wealth
or temporary earthly vain
respect and understanding
are the riches
I seek to gain
for I do know
my life (and yours)
is but a wisp
in an eternal wind
for all I am
is a simple Observer
one lonely soul
ever the grateful server.

Therefore allow me
to share my thoughts
with you the reader again
as you flip through
this page and begin.

Father's Day

My mama wakes me up when I was sleeping in bed. She tells me to get up and wash in the bathroom. Today we are going to see daddy, she said. I was sleepy, but I got out of bed, so mama didn't yell at me. First, I peed and flushed the toilet so mama won't get mad. I brush my teeth and put water in my mouth. Mama walked in to put a wet towel on my face. She woke me up doing that. Mama put the towel under my arms too.

Mama calls me to come into the kitchen. I sat down on a chair. She cooks breakfast on the stove and gives me a plate of toast and bacon. I love toast and bacon, but sometimes when mama makes them with eggs, I don't like them. Mama tells me to eat as much as I can because today we are going to see daddy. When I finish eating my breakfast, mama told me to go to my room and get the suit she bought for me at the store. I go to my room and open the closet. The suit mama gave me is on a hanger. I take it down, and I go to the bathroom, where I put it on. It is a nice suit, said, mama. One that daddy would be proud to see me wear. It has been a long time since I saw daddy. One night I played with my car daddy gave me for my birthday when he told me he was going to the store. I didn't see him after that, and mama never says anything when I ask about daddy. Today I hope to see him.

I put on my suit and go to the living room. I turn on the tee-vee and sit on the sofa. The cartoons are on. Daddy used to watch tee-vee with me all the time. We watch cartoons all the time. Daddy acted like me sometimes. Mama didn't like that. Now I watch cartoons by myself. Mama doesn't like to watch tee-vee, or she did until daddy was gone. She picks me up from school when she is out from her job. Mama walks out of her room. She has on a nice dress and a hat. Mama looks at her watch. She tells me to turn off the tee-vee. My auntie is going to pick us up.

I hear a horn outside the house. My auntie is here. My mama grabs her purse and tells me to come on. I go out the door, and my auntie waits for us in her car. I say 'hi' to my auntie, and she smiles at me when she opens the door. Mama came and opened the back door for me. I put on my seatbelt because she tells me to. As soon as my mama close her door, my auntie's car started moving. We pass by my friend's house. He was riding his bike with his big sister. He saw me wave at him, and I wave back. I want to play with him, but I have gone to see daddy. My mama talks to my auntie. She said she wants to move from where we live because it was getting worse, and she didn't want me to grow up and be a bad person. My daddy used to be a bad person, my mama said. When I was born, he starts turning good.

My auntie drives a long way in her car. We stop at a store. My mama tells my auntie she will be back. When my mama goes inside, my auntie turns around and asks me how I am doing. I say fine, and I tell her I can't wait to see daddy. My auntie turns sad, and I ask her what's wrong. She didn't say anything. Auntie laughs and smiles again. I didn't know why she sad in the first place. Mama came back with some roses. We leave the store.

We stop at this huge place with a big gate on the front. We go through, and I look outside and see a big place with grass and things on the ground. Auntie drives slow, and then we stop. Mama tells me this is it. I go out of the car happy. Daddy is here; I want to see my daddy.

We walk on the grass with the things on the ground. I didn't know why those things are there. They had letters and numbers on them I don't understand. I look for daddy,

12

but I don't see him. I keep asking mama, "Where's daddy? Where's daddy?" She took my hand and said we would see him soon. Mama stop by one of the things on the ground. She lay roses on what my auntie calls a grave. I ask her what does that means, but my auntie doesn't say anything. I start to cry because I don't see daddy. "Daddy's not here!" I tell my mama, "He left me!" Mama gave me a big hug and looked into my eyes. She says daddy isn't with us like I think he is, except he is with us as long as we remember him. I asked mama where is he and mama tells me, "Sweetie, your daddy's in a better place." I ask mama I would ever see him again, she thinks and says "maybe." She says no more. Mama gives me a rose and wants me to put it on his grave.

I think when daddy uses to play with me on the carpet. I wish we played with my cars and watch cartoons again. I ask mama why I never see daddy anymore, and she says a bad man shot him while he was going to the store. I want to cry, but mama gives me another big hug. I turn around and look at my daddy's grave.

I miss you, daddy.

We don't stay too long because mama wants to go home. She takes my hand and leaves the place my auntie call a cemetery. We go back to my auntie's car, and I sit in my seat. Mama sits with me this time. She asks me if I am okay. I tell her yes. I see a tear run down her face. She was crying, but she smiles at me and tell me not to worry, everything will be all right. We are leaving the cemetery, and I remember the last time I see daddy. I wish he was with us now, but I remember him like mama wants me to.

I love you, daddy.

Thank You, Dr. King

Dr. King,
this generation is sorry
you weren't able to cross
the river Jordan with us
but your dream is coming true
and continue it must
for the evil factions
who placed you eternally
underfoot
wish to snatch
the tree of equality
pulling it from its roots.

Fifty-plus years
since you spoke on the podium
in the base of power
declaring your vision
was needed for that hour
fully embraced
in the arms of righteousness
though Man's vices
gave it a test.

You know today in this New Dawn
it's not strange
that a resistant few
cannot accept the change
now, these same forces

use your speeches
bend your words
for their own benefit
but you do know Sir
truth like a sword
severs the dark desires of a man's heart
the dream shall finally prevail
before foolishness
takes a start.

Thank you, Dr. King
for giving our generation
and many more to follow a blueprint
a foundation for peace
that although there will be wars
tranquility will increase
one day this dream
will encompass all
political ideologies cannot stop
this Divine mandate
led by Wisdom herself
who awaits us all
with you standing
at the mountaintop.

We Shall Overcome.

I Don't Understand

"I don't understand."
"I don't understand."
These are the cries
of a collective called Man
they say slavery is over
it didn't end that soon
although physical level
stopped allegedly 1863 June.

"I don't understand."
on a talk show
riotous aftermath
shouts a woman
you really ought to, ma'am
others like yourself lied to
deceived
in the illusion our country
everywhere
had paused with ease
believing years previous
brought peace and prosperity
socially that would be enough
unaware suppressed frustrations later
did passionately erupt.

As you speak into the mike
and your question is grand
repeated from the mouths

of individuals not experienced
in my land
when all they see are
drive-bys, pregnant teens
crack dealers on my block
communal anger, self-rage
media distorts it a lot
narrow sound bites
shown on a small screen
if you ever take time to
visit my land
you'll find the streets
ill-tempered, but not mean.

"I don't understand."
did it come from the lips
of citizens with brooms
secure in hands?
cleaning up South Central
in May 1992
after the explosion
the Fire Next Time blew
hauling off debris
rubble from the unrest
few days before
lone trucker
beaten down senseless
and after all that
could these be the same people
who didn't have a clue

the cause for residents
led by madness out of the blue
no, they could not have been
for these brave souls
took a risk
helping their fellow men
instead of agreeing
with useless myths.

Woman shouts out in frustration
how she doesn't understand
let these words assist at
best as they can
we are all victims
of two-fold mental slavery
Solomon himself even remarked
none escapes captivity
for as long as we remain
content in our ways
satisfied to be isolated
we will never reach full potential
for the cause we were created
myths and lies blind
clear direction
truth eclipsed from our sight
we see through
confused perception
bowing down to old fables
feeling we should question them
reality asks we are able

to not settle for the way
things should always be
for is this not America
home of the brave
land of the free?

Those three words
"I don't understand."
long used as an instrument
for others to justify
Man's endless conquest of Man
the division is his agenda
unity for centuries
never his plan
new century fast approaching
Millennium at the door
this is our greatest quest
to be content or rise for more
finding solutions with haste
in the long run, exceedingly grand
if now we put forth an effort
to listen, learn, and understand.

The Story of Shontell

Shontell was a fast girl
now she's a welfare mother
met up with directionless dudes
spread her legs like peanut butter
she has four kids now
and if you stare closely
at her stomach
while her children laugh and play
you shouldn't be surprised
she has one more
on the way.

Shontell was a good girl
intelligent and oh so smart
pleasing to the eyes too
yet she couldn't fill
the void in her heart
she kept attracting boys
who were only interested
in her booty and chest
she didn't care if they refused
to know the rest
of her.

Now Shontell today
is in her mid-twenties
sitting outside her place
look closely for a second

you'll see a tear dripping down her face
"why does it have to be this way?"
she asks; this isn't what she planned
all she wants and still does
is to be with
an understanding, loving man.

Advice to those
who are growing up
like Shontell
be careful in your
maturing years
for they may be Heaven now
but later on
they may be your private hell.

The Story of the Homeless

Walking downtown, I stare at my feet
an unclean soul lays on hardened concrete
face unwashed, filthy blanket on head
he sleeps on a corner that serves as his bed.

The story of the homeless in our major cities
often to them, we don't show pity
when they plead for just a little change
we glance at them and consider them strange.

I wonder what would happen if roles
are reversed?
The worst becomes better, the better
becomes worst
, and what would we do? Fall on our knees
shouting to Heaven, "Oh please help us, please!"

Another day passes, the homeless still there
in a society that doesn't return a glare
to these people without homes, to them,
we show no pity
but their numbers increase in our major cities.

A Town Called Heaven

Once, a pastor with the best intentions decided he would build a town called Heaven. He allowed all to enter, not discriminating based on race, gender, and social status. Soon the town was full of citizens who all wanted to live there. The pastor required all who entered, wear white as a sign they belonged to the city, nowhere else.

For a time, all was peaceful. Not a foul word or thought was spoken in the confines of the city. Everyone got along and attended the pastor's church he called Sanctuary. Even those who were short of need were assisted by those in the town who had their share. Each Sunday, the townspeople came together to celebrate, worshiping the entire day. However, this would soon come to an end.

A few townspeople questioned the pastor in terms of why they should worship every Sunday. Some preferred a different day, while others wondered why they should gather together with destitute people, accusing them of not doing their fair share in the town. More citizens pondered out loud why they would have to assemble with their fellow townspeople who had a diverse shade of color, even going as far as mentioning they deserve to exclusively wear the white robe, shunning the rest who didn't wear a robe of the same color. Even the robes' subject became an issue as certain townsfolk insisted on donning other colors such as black, brown, yellow, and multicolored. It even reached the point where the townspeople wanted to worship at different times with worshippers they were familiar with.

The pastor watched this unfold in front of his eyes. He felt ill witnessing the divisions among his townspeople. He cautioned Heaven is a place of unity, where all can be one.

Not everyone agreed with his viewpoint. Other men with the name of 'pastor' preached opposing messages insisting Heaven is reserved for one group of people, while the others should leave.

As this raged on, a fire broke out and spread throughout the town, forcing many to flee for safety. The town was soon reduced to nothing more than scorched land, uninhabitable for anyone to live in.

The pastor fell on his knees with tears streaming down his face lamenting the end of his dream. He cried for hours and hours, mourning not only the loss of the town but how it ended. The fire was the final sign all had been lost. Raising his head to the sky, he shouts, "Oh Lord, I tried to create Heaven on earth, I sincerely tried. Now I know for I can see......the folly of it all. Please, forgive me."

He remained there, weeping in silence alone in the middle of the desert, realizing what Man creates, he destroys. Even a replica of the charred remains reminds him of that fact.

I Am Somebody

Hear the call
lead the charge
do something positive
live it large
be someone profound
legendary to the fullest
life isn't always about
dodging or shooting bullets
your soul was originated
from the breath
of the Creator
but it's your choice
to make it even greater.

Yeah, it's true
we all gotta go sometime
sooner than most of us think
Malcolm X, Dr. King
left us in their prime
yet they each
had a mission
attempting to change the ways
of the world
let that be your purpose
for every boy and girl.

Whether you

live in the hood
or far, far away
you can still
keep it real
in your own heart
pave your way
just don't spend
your limited time
in addictive waste
the fruit of greatness
is there before you
go ahead
have a taste.

No matter
if you're young
middle age or old
there's always
a simple chance
to break the mold
becoming just
a tad bit better
perfecting your skill
even if it's sweeping a broom
or sitting down
writing a letter.

"I Am Somebody"
raise your spirit
and your voice

up to the heavens
real loud
don't let others
block your path
walk with royalty
be proud.

When you finally
reach your goal
you can say to yourself
"oh, how good is my soul."
once you do get the height
of the mountain, I do attest
you may have been lost
in the shadows
but you smile
in sunshine
proving to all
that you are the best.

Role Reversal

When I hear people say
they don't have a problem
with a person like me
I nod my head
saying, "good, that's how
it should be"
when it comes down
to something benefiting my race
the same problem
make individuals
do a strange about-face.

They say they weren't responsible
for injustices of the past
an injury America tries to cover
with a conscience filled cast
they say they personally
weren't there
when unjust events went down
it doesn't explain
why Business as Usual
is still around.

Yet such is their right
in a free society
but I don't think it's fair
to blame someone like me

so if I may take a moment
of the reader's fair time
let me be like all the rest
and shout
the fault is not mine!
When you see
an African American
do something terrible on T.V.
why do you automatically
throw them in with me
did I rob your store
hold you at gunpoint
sell any crack
spend time at the joint?
you claim you're not responsible
for past atrocities
they why in the world
Do you spin present ones at me?
why am I guilty
because I wear
the same outfits outlaws adorn
not all people of color toot
the same horn.

Why do you look at me
with suspicion in the air
you think I beat up
someone with privileged skin?
oh no Sir, I wasn't there
you say you don't condone

the actions of a few
(who belong to your race)
so maybe you think for
a quick minute
that I might agree with you?

Perhaps I've never done wrong
but when you smell my scent
you act as if I have
a criminal aroma
too bad
you'll never find out
I graduated with honors
when I received my diploma.
Think about it for a moment
if you want to be fair
don't compare me
with the 'thugs' you see over there
if you don't want a debate
to turn controversial
then afford me the same benefit
of the doubt
when it comes to your
role reversal.

The Party

There they were. Five souls whose blood was spilled on a cold, dirty pavement of a South Central Los Angeles sidewalk. News teams from local television stations cover the tragic event armed with on-field reporters holding microphones and cameras; paramedics healing wounded survivors, police interview the rest not within in the line of fire. They speak with residents in the neighborhood willing to discuss the shooting to a point, at least the ones who agreed to talk openly under a cloud of anonymity.

"Did you see what happened?" A policeman scribbles notes next to a young woman with a caramel complexion sitting on the front lawn, grieving her friends' loss. Her eyes release anguished tears running down her cheek, lamenting the sudden deaths. Her spirit feels as it was snatched from her body, realizing the significance of the heartbreak. She recalls her tragic tale to the tall Caucasian uniformed officer vainly trying to calm her down—other young people surviving the assault weep uncontrollably. At the same time, a few shook their heads in disgust. Neighbors surrounding the crime scene's aftermath were left to mutter in sullen whispers, only in South Central.

Although few of the uniformed officers present were professional, there are at least two in their camp leaning up against a squad car asking, "Where's Black Lives Matter? Why aren't they're here? These lives mattered too!" One officer speaks his question loud enough for everyone around him to hear. An older black gentleman wearing a tee shirt with the tail hanging below the belt challenges the officer with angry words as he creeps closer to the edge of his front lawn.

"These children are dead, and you have the nerve to ask about Black Lives Matter?" He speaks in a deep, authoritative voice. The officer turns his head in the gentleman's direction but reverses it towards his partner with indifference.

"Aw, forget it." The officer quickly ends a potentially heated confrontation, taking away the gravity from the evening's tragedy. The older gentleman grunts, displeased at the officer's ill remark. Witnessing the result of the aftermath he shakes his head, and decides to stay outside to absorb the egregious losses of life near his home. It is an unfortunate custom he has been forced to become accustomed to since his family moved into this neighborhood nearly fifty years ago.

The media crews on-site gather information for their television and newspaper reports. This recent heartbreak may be featured on the daily newspaper's front page or the very last blurb on a website. If they choose to, masses of people will reluctantly digest the senseless slaughter in the South area of the city and may never give it a second thought. Activists and law enforcement spokespersons will condemn the event, while neighbors burned out by the useless killings will just accept it as a fact of life, the way things are. At any rate, the five souls whose lives were taken from indiscriminate bullets of a drive-by shooting will never return to life again.

For the ones who survived the carnage, the clock turns back on this night full of laughter, fun, peace, and tragedy.

The night of the party.

It was intended to be a sendoff party for Calvin Clemons. Calvin, an all-city, all-state tailback who attends a local high school in the community, will travel to Montana West University the following week to register for classes and meet with the football coach. He was heavily recruited by a few prominent colleges and universities in the country, such as UCLA, Georgia, Grambling, and Rutgers, before deciding on Montana West.

A residential house in the neighborhood hosted the party with numerous African American and Latino youth, all present to wish Calvin a fond farewell. The deejay hired for this special occasion carefully mixes selected songs on his laptop, connected to the amplified sounds of his four foot sound speakers: Janae the hostess, hands two of her guests a plate filled with chips and dip. An attractive young woman set to graduate with Calvin has many admirers. Her luscious caramel skin tone shines in the moonlight. She possesses a stunning shapely build with a body older women would envy. Her denied suitors know she belongs to one person, Calvin. That isn't to say she doesn't have trusted male friends. One of them, a short and thin confidante named Alfonso taps her on her shoulder. With a wide grin, he flashes a smile made prominent by his butter pecan complexion.

"Hey, Janae, what's up?" He speaks with a Latin accent, checking out the green dress she wears.

"What up, Alfonso? Glad you made it." She smiles, placing her arms around her childhood friend dressed to impress in his button-down shirt, with a friendly hug.

A loud voice booms behind Janae. "Aw, you hug this punk and don't even say 'hi' to your man?" Turning around, Janae notices Alfonso's companion, taller with a set of broad shoulders very noticeable under the shirt he wears.

It was Calvin.

"Yeah, I see you 'He-Man,' give me a kiss." Janae and Calvin embrace each other with locked lips, giggling as they commit the act.

Alfonso watches the two happily getting along. There was a time when they were younger, he developed feelings

33

for Janae but lost out to Calvin because he liked her more and vice versa. The couple had been together for a year and a half, and little thoughts of marriage snuck in their passionate conversations. The parents of the young lovers believe they were far too young for such a lifelong commitment. Nevertheless, Janae and Calvin kept a strong bond, and they weren't about to let each other go. If it means waiting three or four years, so be it. Calvin is also best friends with Alfonso. Although he will miss Calvin, Alfonso privately hopes Calvin might forget all about her so that he finally might have an opportunity with Janae and share his inner feelings on how much he likes her. He really understands that could never be, so he left that foolish suggestion alone. His mind is on a more severe matter involving her that needs to be discussed.

Moments later, the crowd of young people is fired up dancing to the deejay's fast songs, motivating them to join in the middle of the wooden living room floor which serves as the dance area. After everyone moves to the beat, three Black youths enter through the front door. One is tall with a thin build, dressed in a tee-shirt and blue jeans. Lamar is his name. Ronald, the second person in the bunch, stands at five feet, ten inches, proudly wearing his school's baseball jersey and pants. A Dodgers baseball cap, plain shirt, and jeans distinguish the third youngster Lonshay, a tad shorter than his friends. He has a small, robust physical frame. Certain boys who tried to mess with him learned their error via hurt feelings and sore body parts. Calvin pointed to his tall friend and shouted, "Lamar, go home son! This is for grown folks!"

Lamar fires back, "What the hell you doing here then? You ain't that grown!"

Calvin laughs. "Now see, y'all starting mess at my party with all these lame jokes." He bumps fists with

Lamar. He hugs Calvin in return. "I wanted to clown you one more time before you left, you sorry sap."

Near the snack table by the kitchen, Ronald holds a bagful of chips in his hand. Alfonso passes by. "Dang Ronald, save me some." Janae taps Alfonso on the shoulder. "May I talk to you?" The agreeable young man made no complaints. He follows her away from the crowd, outside to the backyard. They meet inside the garage without being spotted. Janae has a troubled look on her face. Alfonso is equally concerned.

"Did you tell him yet?" He asked.

Janae reacts by shaking her head no.

Alfonso throws up his hands. "When are you going to tell him? He'll be on that plane in a few days and it'll be too late."

"You don't understand." She snaps. Janae folds her arms across her body staring anxiously at the ground. She remains quiet for a minute then speaks. "I'm afraid….afraid if I tell him, he may never come back. I'm also afraid he'll find another girl, a prettier one out there where he's going, and forget all about me. If he finds a white girl.........oh, that will kill me more."

"No, he won't. He loves you."

"How can you be so sure?"

"Janae if you just tell him, I'm sure he'll understand. Trust me, please. I'm his best friend." Alfonso holds out his hands. He possesses the urge to reach out further to emphasize his point. Or perhaps through some desperate final fantasy, he wishes she accepts his open arms and hides her inside for comfort. Alas, it was only just a fantasy. Reality stares him right in the face.

Janae walks over to the far side of the darkened garage, agonizing with her decision. Finally, she replied, "I... I will. Before the night's over, I'll tell him." One brief pause later, tears begin to fill her eyes. She pleads to Alfonso. "Hold me, please."

He responds to her request, smiling as soon it is fulfilled.

Two hours later, inside the crowded house, the intensity of the fast music takes its course. The deejay decides to switch the mood and resorts to playing slow songs. One in particular is *Always and Forever* by the R&B group Heatwave. In the minds of many, it is the ultimate love song. Janae and Calvin close their eyes, listening to the words. Their bodies are in tune with each other, hips sway from side to side. Janae's passionate hands press behind her boyfriend's buttoned-down shirt, tempting him to rip it off his body. Calvin lays his hands on her hips. He desires her to the point he longs to touch and taste the great treasures of his lady. Each gazes into the other's eyes, remembering the importance of the relationship, the commitment they both share romantically. This was love taking over.

By the time the slow jams were finished, the deejay decides to take a break. The large crowd socializes in the living room. Young men with plans charming females met their lustful goals by securing phone numbers of interested ladies. Others converse with friends, either outside the porch or in the backyard, enjoying the calmness of the evening, the celebration for one of their own on his way to being a success, a feat seldom achieved in this area of the city. The two lovers sit down on the living room couch. Calvin's muscular arm wraps around his woman, blushing. Sitting in a group near the front of the sofa are Lamar, Alfonso, Ronald, and Janae's best friend, a petite young woman with a smooth caramel complexion. It isn't hard to notice her, with a long strand of hair flowing in the back.

"Man, I can't believe you, Janae, and Alfonso going out in the real world. Now that you about to graduate, how do you feel? Happy?" Ronald addresses Calvin. Alfonso replies, "I don't know how the lovebirds feel, but I'm glad I don't have to be in that teacher's English class anymore."

"Yeah, everybody hates his class because he's too boring. He mumbles a lot, and you can't hear what he's saying. Dang, I got him next year too!" Lamar cringes at the thought. Janae's friend poses a serious question. "Calvin, Janae, you're going to be far away from each other. Are you two going to keep in touch?"

Janae stares right at Calvin. "I don't know, will we?"

Calvin flashes a grin. "Of course baby girl, you know I love you." He smiles affectionately towards her. Feeling her doubts temporarily evaporate, Janae kisses her man on the cheek. He returns the favor by kissing her on the forehead. Aware they were making a scene, the couple stops smooching. Attention is being drawn to them.

"Hmm, don't stop on our account." Janae's friend giggles, placing a hand over her mouth. Alfonso sitting a few feet from the couch has a different thought.

I wonder if she told him yet?

A young Latino gentleman with a thick muscular build and a teammate of Calvin steps to the side with car keys in hand. "Say, bro, I'm about to leave, and I think your car is blocking mine."

"Hey, no sweat. Come on, and I'll move mine." Calvin grabs his keys and steps outside. "I'll go out with you." Alfonso accompanies his best friend out the door. Janae's heart skips a beat suspecting Alfonso may tell Calvin what they kept secret. Minutes after, the two young men stand on the foot of the concrete steps in the front of the walkway leading up to the porch. Calvin takes a minute to stare at the black starlit sky above them. "Check them out."

"What?" Alfonso asks.

"The stars, I mean…they're so much like life," Calvin explains with a philosophical view uncommon at his age.

37

"People say reach for the stars, and you'll be a success, right?" He pauses. "I wasn't going for them at all. I only wanted to work hard enough so the team could go into the playoffs and win the city. We came close, and all. Dorsey was a great opponent, but as far as the awards and stuff? Man, I didn't even expect that."

Alfonso laughs. "Just shows what hard work, dedication, and good friends are all about, success."

"Yeah, I guess. But you know, when I make the pros, the first thing I'm gonna do is to get my mama and two sisters out of here. They don't deserve to live with all these shootings, drugs, and stuff. Then if I get richer, I'm gonna build a huge sports complex right here in the hood. That'll be something the community will like. Man, I tell you that I want the little kids to be proud to say they live down here one day. I want a kid to stick out his chest, hold his head up high and say, "I'm from South Central", and not even worry what folks think about him or her. When I start football practice at Montana West, I'm gonna look a linebacker in the eye, run him over and say, 'that's for the hood.' Calvin grins.

"You already made the first step, dude, college." Alfonso continues to listen to his friend, leaning back. "But you do know if you move your family out, some white family will just move in here. I heard that's happening a lot now."

"So what?" Calvin shrugs his shoulders, not caring for his friend's future scenario. "Let them. I don't care. As long as my folks are out of here, I'm good. As far as what you're saying about college, I'm just taking the path my mama took, you know? I'm gonna get an education too, so other people will know just because you come from a black and brown neighborhood, it doesn't mean you're stupid, killing your kind, or selling dope. That's what I'm gonna do." Calvin looks solemnly at the ground, sticking his

38

hands deep inside his pockets. "What about you? What do you plan to do with your life?" Calvin turns towards him. Alfonso pauses for an answer. "I might go to a junior college next year and transfer to either Cal-State L.A. or U.S.C. and major in business. Wherever I go, I plan to be a success just like you, big man!" Calvin laughs, happy his best friend has plans for his direction in life.

"There you go, Alfonso! One thing about stars, if you have goals and dreams, they ain't too far to reach."

"What about Janae? Is she in your plans too?" Alfonso stares at his friend, awaiting an answer regarding their relationship status. Until now, Alfonso didn't get the answer he wanted to hear. This time, he did.

"Yes indeed. I love her. I love Janae with all my heart. No matter what happens, she'll be mine till the end." It was a sincere heartfelt reply from the young Black man, a response that just about answered all questions Alfonso had for both of them. He feels relieved that although he'll always admire Janae from afar, he knows she's with a good man. As long as she's happy, Alfonso can live with that knowledge.

Janae, who overheard the conversation, walks outside to sit with the two young men. "You two are missing the party. Come back inside."

"Don't worry; we will. We're just talking about the future and stars and stuff." Calvin tells her, winking to his lady.

"Uh, I think I better go back inside." Alfonso excuses himself. In his thoughts, he surmises, "At least they're alone. Now she can tell him."

Before another word could be said, the sound of screeching tires slamming against the asphalt of city streets halts any thoughts of conversation as words spoken in profane tones are shouted from the unrepentant voices of phantoms. Alfonso turns his body around, noticing a shining, gleaming object signaling the end of life and the coming of death from a passing car.

"Oh, Lord!" Alfonso's eyes widen.

It was too late.

Blasts from the shotgun of the speeding vehicle shock those inside the house, resorting to quick action. Party participants duck instantly to the floor. Janae's mother frantically looks around and realizes her daughter isn't in the place. Her lips release a shrill cry. "Janae! Janae!"

The shooting doesn't last long, maybe thirty seconds. However, time was of no consequence as a dreadful silence permeates the air, capturing the essence of the people's shattered nerves inside the house. Lamar was the first brave soul to step outside and what he discovered was very disheartening. Bullet holes were found on the house walls. The windows with gated bars were shattered. Five people were gunned down. Three young people leaving the party early are found dead in the driveway. No life could be seen or felt in them, for they were killed without remorse, without reason. Lamar gazes in horror as fresh blood pours out of the victims' warm bodies. Tears swell in his eyes. He knew they had passed on.

Like Janae.

Like Calvin.

Both had held hands together till the end.

Lamar hears muffled sounds beneath him. A hand covered in crimson taps his right ankle. Alfonso still lives, choking up blood. Lamar shouts out, "Call for an ambulance! Hurry!" Barely alive, Alfonso slowly observes the riddled bodies of dead friends.

Solemnly, he wept.

Janae's mother did not contain herself bursting out of the house dashing toward her lifeless daughter. Frail arms of the older Black woman cradle her sweet baby's lifeless head. "Janae! My baby! Oh sweet Jesus, my baby!" Her

40

heart cries out in agony as her child's lifeblood ruthlessly drips to the concrete below. Deep inside, she knows there was nothing else she could do. There was nothing anyone could do.

Field news crews covering the tragedy were long gone. The police left to start their investigation of the shooting. A crowd that shortly swelled after the police helicopters and cars arrived began to diminish. Caring neighbors console the grieving families knowing whatever they did in word or deed wouldn't make a difference. Friends of the deceased hug each other; fortunate, they avoided the horrific fate of the evening. The same survivors weep for Calvin and Janae, feeling losses only they can explain. The paramedics remain to tend to those seriously wounded, such as Alfonso.

A lone paramedic tells him laying on a stretcher, "One bullet passed through your leg and another lodged in your shoulder but consider yourself lucky. You'll live." Alfonso speaks under his breath with a tone of bitterness. "Yeah, damn lucky."

Lamar steps by his side. "Alfonso.........." He tries to speak with choked words too hard to come out. "You all right? You gonna be okay?"

Alfonso slowly shakes his head, closing his eyes. He turns towards Lamar with regret. "She didn't even tell him. Janae didn't tell Calvin she...she was six weeks pregnant with his child." The paramedics load Alfonso into the ambulance, tears streak down his face. His heart increases in heavy grief. It will be grief he, Lamar, and everyone involved will feel for a long, long time.

There they were. Five souls who had their blood spilled on the pavement of a South Central Los Angeles sidewalk. Loves, friendships, and dreams died this night, as is often the case in tragedies such as this. To the world at large, they will be nothing but mere statistics. To the survivors, this is a night that will not be soon forgotten, for this was the night of the party.

In All Fairness

Ladies
you have requirements
for the men
trust us completely
we do understand
but please don't be offended
when we make the same demands
all we ask
no, insist in all things
of the heart
be fair
we will treat you like royalty
though we're distant
from being real heirs.

That's all we request
it's only right and just
we may not possess a kingdom
it is our hope
you'll see the wealth
we're willing to share inside of us.

A Piece of Wisdom

Wisdom herself
throughout the centuries
with her own eyes
witnesses Man's cruelty
injustice blowing
freely through time's wind
even here in America
where it never
seems to end.

She has seen
men of truth rise up
destined to violently
lay down
Humanity, in his foolishness
refuses to hear
her sweet righteous sound.

Wisdom is a peaceful spirit
she grants noble men the ability
to think and decipher
knowledge as she lends
faithful others shall be like her
instructing Man
the correct steps
he must undertake
to be bonded
by the light of truth

a new path of justice
common sense must create.

Evil never lasts
it doesn't prevail for long
because its vision is impaired
sincere men
shall see that working hard
ensuring may all things be fair
others will rise
taking the place
of the slain
ringing out
the call for freedom
to fresher ears
all over again.

I'm Proud

I'm proud
proud to have you
as my lady
for all the times
you said "you will"
when I hesitated
with "maybe."
you truly accept me
in everything I say and do
from solitary beach walks
to taking fun pictures
at the local park
yes, baby, for sure
I do love you.

Sin Is In

In a New York office high atop the metropolitan city, a group of advertising executives is figuring out a way to market a brand new soda. Although not too controversial, the name was certain to raise just a few eyebrows, especially in the Bible Belt. Interestingly enough, the owner of the company (he calls it De Monic Enterprises) made sure it had a distinct name for everyone to take notice of. He calls it Sin.

Now provocative names are nothing new when it comes to brand names on merchandise such as lingerie. Even the pop star Madonna published a book called Sex, so these ad execs are tapping fingers on desks, fiddling with their pens, scrolling for websites on the internet (even those they were warned NOT to look at), ponder what and how they would market this delicious but challenging product to the masses. Suddenly, they made a decision which they felt they had no choice but to go with.

They went ahead and marketed the soda anyway.

Within a matter of weeks, the advertising firm produced a gigantic blitz on all forms of media. Everyone given the commercials, whether on regular television or the internet, witnessed what they saw. However, the commercials' producers did their utmost best to convince everyone what they watched and heard wasn't real. A group of young people at a party did unlawful acts; smoking drugs, prostituting, hurting each other. The actions depicted in the commercials were justified as the people on screen or the web drank from the soda. In a way, they were enticing, attractive to the naked eye, and viewers, for the most part, could forgive what they watched. For example, here are a few quotes from the ads:

"Sin gets you into places you've never dreamed of!"

"Sin is cool!"

"Sin is not boring!"

"If you want to get ahead in the world, Sin is the way to go!"

"Sin is for the in-crowd homies!"

"Sin gives you the ability to be Number One! Forget the rest because they don't run with you anyway. Leave those losers alone!"

"Sin is so rad, dude! You should try it!" Says a dude dressed in a tank top and shorts on a beach wearing sunglasses eyeing a woman's crotch taking a sip.

"Don't worry what the haters say; Sin is in!" A young woman sells her body for her pimp while drinking from a can.

"Everybody drinks it, everybody." An athlete recites his lines with wide eyes as he tilts his head back for a sip of his own.

Sin had become so popular, it outsold every soda on the market; Pepsi, Coke, no cola producer was left standing in Sin's wake. It was political leaders, celebrities, even down to the regular middle and lower class citizens who indulged in the beverage. Sin had not only overtaken the market; everyone in the world enjoyed the delicious, enticing soda.

Across the street, marketers of a different ad company proposed to counter Sin with an alternative called Salvation. The challenge of marketing the brand was how to make it more appealing to the younger set. They came up with a strategy to present their lifestyle by drinking their new but safe product. One more wholesome, productive, and drama-free. There were no wanton acts of degradation, no shock value involved, just pure unadulterated freshness in a can the second marketing company hoped to convey for its owner, Miss Ann Jelick. Unfortunately, the majority didn't appreciate the taste of Salvation, opting to remain with their favorite drink instead. Even the marketing company who produced the award-winning ads for Sin revealed a new set of commercials, which made fun of its competitor:

"Who cares about Salvation? Old, boring, and it ain't cool!"

"Nothing compares to Sin, not even a watery drink like Salvation! Sin has a smooth taste and more!"

"I wouldn't be caught dead with Salvation! No way, bruh; Sin is number one, and it'll always be that way!"

As one would expect, Sin continued its dominance in the marketplace. At the same time, Salvation was nearly wiped out by the competition and may have disappeared altogether had it not been for one major flaw in Sin's chemical composition. The "side effects" weren't noticeable at first due to the massive purchases worldwide. It appeared De Monic Enterprises had lied - yes, lied - about the astronomical amount of sodium in their soft drinks. Although their labels said otherwise, the truth is that Sin had three times the regular amount of their competitors, blended in with extra corn syrup to add to the "juicy" flavor. Before too long, users' complaints with extraordinary amounts of high blood pressure, diabetes, and even fatalities were linked to Sin.

Due to public pressure, the makers of Sin and the advertising company faced their day in court. The advertising agency was found guilty with documents stating they knew the real illegal content in the soda, but somehow De Monic Enterprises was found not guilty of any charges. Sin as a soft drink ceased to exist after that, but the damage in the aftermath of users racking up high hospital bills was done.

In the end, Salvation ended up the clear winner in the so-called "new cola wars" but still found a negative stigma applied to the brand. Former users of Sin still didn't believe its competitor was the safer alternative, preferring the taste of Sin although it wasn't around on the shelves much longer. In an ironic twist, the lead manager for the advertising company that helped promote the soda died. At his funeral, two of his assistants stood near the casket before it was lowered six feet below the ground forever. One of the assistants turned to the other, quoting a familiar biblical scripture.

"I guess it is true; the wages of Sin is death." To which the other assistant nods his head and replies,

"But it made us rich, didn't it?"

Bang! Bang!

Back in 1991
in the Southside
a young girl's life
ended with the discharge of a gun
a shot heard far and wide
around the hood
prejudiced court decreed
her existence on earth
was invalid, no good.

A few years later
in a town called Riverside
Nineteen shots fired
on a young lady
fatally piercing
her dark hide.

In New York City
legendary for
infamous crimes
added another one
when an innocent
was crucified by the bullet
forty-one times.

These shots weren't
fired by hoodlums

thugs and their kind
rather they were released
by individuals
whose backgrounds
boggle the mind
authorities, store owners
all were pulling the trigger
on the quick
young lives taken
from this earth
lights out, that's it.

Fighting evil with evil
in our Wild West American society
offers no restitute
trigger happy justice
maybe winked at
morally offers no absolute
however
as long as this is permissible
by those seated
in the thrones of power
these tragedies
continue to mount
even in this eleventh hour.

Almighty Dollar

It has been said
a fool and his gold
are soon parted
even worse
than a jilted lover
breaking down brokenhearted
of a mate, they know
will never be seen again
so it is
when a miser
loses his gain.

Of course
this piece isn't about
positive folks
blessed with wealth
from their hearts, they give
no, this is meant
for undesirables
and the wanton life they live
pumped up full
of arrogant self-pride
you may floss
in an empty shell
but the soul rots on the inside.

Lust of money
plus lust of the flesh
slow and creeping
long term moral death
relish in your power
revel in your glory
when it's your turn
to sleep in the ground
all that remains
is another sad story.

What does the youth hear?
what are the images they view
our kids are led
by many pied pipers
on the verge
of disappearing too
'substance is power.'
a message to the children
from individuals, they can relate
to be recognized as human beings
a promising treasure
shall validate.

I'd wish they see
Central High School
marches in the South
Sit-Ins
led by their elders
folks and other kin

making a stand
freedom and equality
it wasn't only for their time
but for the next generation
meaning you and I
and for those
who may scoff
messages of this poetic flow
those riches you love
wouldn't be obtained as fast
had not folks ended
physical Jim Crow.

21st Century
just trying to holla
out to you peeps
in love with
the almighty dollar
now money's good
when it's applied
this is the hour
we in Black skin
can turn the social tide
use what you've earned wisely
spend it to help
someone else
should this moment pass
and no gains are made
there would be no one to blame
but ourselves.

I'm not saying
don't enjoy your paper
only dropping two cents
in the cup
hoping you'll use it
for purpose greater
please be careful with
what you earn
each one of us must do the same
a lesson, sooner or later
everyone will learn.

Don't Judge
a Bum by...

A couple of African American women in their early thirties casually stroll down First Street and Grand in the heart of downtown Los Angeles with newly constructed skyscrapers in the distance. One of the women wears a sports coat, a skirt, and lace stockings covering her butter pecan skin. She possesses an indistinguishable hairstyle as she walks down the sidewalk. Her associate with a darker skin shade is dressed in a bright-colored low-cut blouse, skirt, and high heels. Her lips shine with bright crimson, sporting a short haircut. The two petite yet attractive young ladies pass a pleasant dashing fellow in Aaron Monroe. He flashes a polite smile; they respond by quickly turning their heads in the other direction. Their eyes continue to look forward, not giving him a second thought, although he wears an appealing casual outfit with a clean shaved face and head. Even his new casual shoes have a stylish appeal. Both ladies slowly diminish from sight. Bitterly Aaron shakes his head, prompting him to part his lips within earshot, "The Black woman."

"What do you mean, Aaron?" His friend, Daniel, is similarly dressed but is shorter in stature beside Aaron. He curiously asks what he meant by his last comment. The two men had completed another grinding workday, waiting under a hot blazing sun for their bus shuttle to arrive. Their destination is the Metro Rail Station on Flower and Seventh Street.

"Daniel, don't you get sick and tired hearing African American women can't find enough *good* black men. If by chance they do find their "Mr. Right", they whine and complain these men aren't good enough because they're either too short, don't drive an expensive car, not making anything past six figures, etc. It's not like every brother can play pro ball or have a grip of money. I guarantee they'll lie to your face swearing up and down, "It's not true! It's not true!" when you know damn well it's the truth." Aaron protests. "I mean, dang! What does a black man have to do to hook up with a sista today? Sign a contract?"

"Aaron, I think you're blowing this way out of proportion." Daniel cautions, holding his hands in the air. "Not all Black women are like that, I'm sure. The ones who are picky choosing their men are the same ones who will miss out on finding a good man in the long run."

"And just who are the picky ones, you ask? The fine-looking gals, that's who. I tell you my brother, women enjoy one common denominator, money. The days a woman liked you for your mind is dead, believe that! Today you can be the greatest, smartest, most understanding Black man, but if you're poor as spit struggling to make it, forget that. I mean, the Black woman is interested in three things; C.P.A. M.B.A, and N.B.A. And they stay away from any brother investigated by the D.E.A. if you get my drift."

Daniel is quite aware his friend was harsh with his tone. "Aaron look; why do you believe the Black woman today is so vicious? There are a few sistas who are the opposite of what you're portraying them to be. For example, a few women claim that all men are dogs, but take a look at us. We don't smoke, drink excessively, or sell drugs. What else is there to prove we're not as they picture us to be?"

"I'm five foot nine, and you're five foot five. See, some twisted sista is out there dissing 'y'all too short.' You want to know something else that ticks me off? Their high and mighty, don't care for brothers, selfish, childish, stuck up attitude. What's the meaning of it? Dog, the way these sistas snap their fingers, you'd think they get blisters."

Daniel keeps silent, lowering his head to avoid expected agitated stares of Black women passing by. However, he is grateful no one is around to take Aaron's constant rambling seriously. "But that's all right because I can play that game too. Check this out." Aaron opens his backpack revealing two hundred lottery tickets. Daniel saw the numbers on the dockets, Quick Pick and Scratchers his friend hold in his possession. "The Super Jackpot rose to seven hundred million last week. I'm dead certain I will win when they announce the numbers tonight. I went to that liquor store in Hawthorne, the one where people win all the time just because they bought lottery tickets there? Anyway, when I win and become famous, all of these Black women who didn't like me before, I'll flash my dollar bills into their poor cold little puppy dog eyes and say, 'Sorry babe, you don't meet my standards.' Yeah, I'll laugh in their faces too. I tell you, I'll be sharp. Shoot, I'll be too hard for a MasterCard."

Daniel lets Aaron continue. He knows it's hopeless, pointless getting through to his friend with common sense, so he allows him to keep ranting and raving his message of bitterness, hoping the shuttle bus will arrive on time. He thinks how sad one or two broad generalizations of the Black woman stereotype affected Aaron in this manner. Daniel understands Aaron just broke up from a bad relationship (Aaron's girlfriend broke up with him on less than mutual terms and eventually married another man shortly after that) and how that influences his recent view of Black women. *We may never understand each other, but there are some good women out there.* Daniel reflects in deep thought. He holds a decent job as a mail clerk for a prestigious law firm while Aaron works in a coffeeshop as a barista a block away from the office. Finally, their shuttle arrives at the stop in the nick of time, according to Daniel. It will be a miracle if Aaron's diatribe stops at that moment but to no avail. He continues his critical assault inside the shuttle right before the end of their stop.

"Black women are like a compass; they go any which way the wind blows. Now I told you they only appreciate three types, to which we belong to none of them, but they are also turning towards them T.W.A.'s, Thugs with Attitude. Another prime example of why sistas are so confused today."

"Oh no," Daniel shakes his head, burying it in his hands, not believing every new accusation that flows from his friend's mouth.

"In reality, Black women say they don't want a boring man, a wimp, whatever. When they meet their dream thug, I mean man, who doesn't take any lip from a confused female – these women would have you believe their rights are violated. For example, if it came down to where they were going to have dinner, the thug chooses Pizza Hut while his woman wants to go to Gladstone's; who do you think is going to win that argument?"

"I assume they will compromise and go to a restaurant or an all-you-can-eat place that has both, right?" Daniel surmises.

"Wrong again, my naive friend! Pizza Hut wins every time! In some cases, Mickey D's! If the thug wants pizza, dang skippy, he's having pizza, and there's nothing the Black woman can do about it! Oh, she may cry and go 'boo hoo, hoo, I can't go to Gladstone's', but deep down inside, she knows she has to be with this man because she doesn't want to admit she's with the wrong dude, a guy she thought was her Prince Charming."

"Oh, come on!" Daniel throws up his hands. "You mean to tell me that his woman couldn't express her feelings about going to the places she wants to go, the things she wants to do with him? This thug has to have a total say?"

"Yeah." Aaron smiles, laughing. "You know why? It's all part of that Catwoman complex, the dang duality they have. They love hanging with the thug or a brother with a C.P.A., but deep down, they can't stand his butt. Even if they have the most incredible sex, she still gets confused about whether she wants this guy or not. It's all in that new book I read, Real Men Weep In the Basement, by this writer, Carlos Cheatham. He is laying it down and telling the truth about these Black women saying how they can't play the victim role if they don't know what they want or who they want. I say, right on Carlos!"

"Carlos Cheatham? Isn't he the one who wrote those romance poems and novels years ago? Man, he must have seriously changed after his divorce. It's almost the same situation you went through when your ex broke up with you!"

"Brother Man said it wasn't about that, and it ain't about that stink butt girl too! Cheatham wrote in his book that he woke up and realized no matter what, Black women are always going to trip. They could have the next Dr. Martin Luther King Junior, a good man, a solid man, and a stable man. But then they trip and say they bored going after someone one hundred eighty degrees different than the man they are looking for. It's all in the book!" Daniel shakes his head back and forth. Now he discovers the origin of Aaron's extreme ideals.

The injured leading the blind.

"I'm sure the women don't agree with all or anything he says. I mean, it's all a gimmick to sell his books, right? Whatever controversy you can get, use it."

"Yeah, you would think these women would raise a fuss at his book signings and seminars, but like the man says, sistas either trip or give lip, but they'll show up by the dozens and buy his book, so who's wrong now? If they only swallow their pride and admit it, they'll find out brothas like Cheatham and I are for real. They just can't handle it."

"It's a good thing we're inside a shuttle headed towards our train."

"Why? I ain't scared of them, especially those confused, crazy types!"

"Not that, but I would be afraid of lightning bolts striking you down from the sky railing on sistas like that!"

"You just scared of the lip!"

Aaron continues his hysterical tirade as he and Daniel descend on the Seventh and Flower Metro Rail station's steps. The two wade through a crowd of people who were finished with their workday. In plain view rests the southbound Blue Line train on the tracks. Its destination is the Wardlow station in Long Beach. There were two empty chairs in one car not filled.

Both men rush to those empty seats before they were claimed. Daniel sits by a Latino gentleman, fading off to sleep. Aaron takes an uncomfortable seat by an elderly white male in a torn shirt, ripped casual pants, and dirty black hair underneath a severely stained baseball cap. His shoes are worn out completely. The odor emitting from his body has a sour smell. Aaron finds himself fortunate in a sarcastic way to sit next to this person. He responds by whispering, "Phew." He makes facial expressions to Daniel focused on a neatly dressed Black woman in a navy blue suit with a briefcase in hand. She checks her smartphone for the time, wishing the train leave at its scheduled time. With a bit of courage, He rises from his seat and introduces himself across the way in a seat available next to her.

Aaron wishes he could follow his friend's lead and move somewhere else. His legs are too tired from standing, and there isn't another seat available on the rapidly crowded railcar. Since Aaron didn't have to wait too long before his stop, he decides to stick it out. *This old bum isn't going to do anything, so why trip?* Thought Aaron. The disheveled old man slightly turns his head to ask Aaron a question. "Hello, how are you?"

Aaron is taken aback, not expecting the old man to speak, replies with a slight "Hi." He shakes his head. *This man looks like he played 'Wheel of Roaches' and won.* Aaron laughs to himself with that passing thought. Once again, the elder speaks. "I know what you're thinking. This sure is a dirty old man in the literal sense, and you're right. But you know, it's not my fault I'm homeless and penniless. I mean, everything was going right between Francesca and me until we broke up."

Dog, now he's starting to talk to me. Aaron turns up his nose due to the smell. His mother reminded him at an early age angels often appear in strange guises. Shaking his head, the young Black man is convinced the stranger next to him is not one of them. *Naw, no angel would look as bad as a homeboy.* Aaron is quite a veteran of public transportation. He recalls from experience there are many individuals who 'need help' and happen to find their way to a bus or train at all times of the day. So he knows what to expect; he just isn't ready for it today of all days. When the old man begins to speak of his condition, Aaron is drawn to the conversation. Due to his own past relationship problems, he could relate.

"Francesca, was she your girlfriend, wife..." Aaron pauses, beginning to show some interest.

"My ex-wife. By the way, my name is John." He offers his hand to Aaron, but the young man refuses, not sure of the places the hand has surfaced.

"Okay, John, how did she leave you?"

"She ran away." The old man reveals.

"Oh really?" Aaron begins a curiosity, anxious to learn more.

"See, things weren't right in our marriage, and she left me for a younger stud. Now I'm town trying to find her."

Aaron is a bit puzzled. "Your ex-wife ran off on you, and now you're trying to find her?"

"That's right." John nods his head in agreement, lips tucked under a gray beard.

"Why? I would have let her go. I'm just honest. No woman that picks another man over you is worth it. Especially an uppity Black woman who thinks she's the spit." Aaron interjects his view of the matter.

"Well, my wife didn't run off with a man; she ran off with a stud." John tries to correct Aaron.

"Stud, bud, whatever. Like the saying goes, gotta go, gotta go."

Aaron turns his attention towards Daniel, involved in a deep conversation with the woman next to him. A disapproving frown forms on Aaron's face, hoping his friend wouldn't have him heartbroken by this no-good woman out for money.

"And that's it? I always wondered what Atlanta is like." Daniel smiles at the attractive woman with an intoxicating caramel complexion wearing eyeglasses beside him. She appears studious, intelligent. Daniel observes the smooth facial features of his traveling companion. She is pleasing to his eyes as he is to hers.

"Uh, brother, excuse me for a minute. Did you hear this old man next to me? He claims he's from out of town looking for his wife, who left with a 'stud.' Now I don't know about you, but…"

Daniel cuts off his buddy in mid-sentence to say, "Aw Aaron, that's rude. Here I am engaged in a positive conversation with this fine Black sista. You know, the very women you claim to be the scourge of our existence? So while you're complaining about that guy next to you, at least let me keep talking with Felicia, and you can finish your discussion with that crazy man."

Aaron seems displeased with Daniel's reaction. "It's like that, huh? You turned into the Black Benedict Arnold of manhood! Hey, it's your dignity and respect. Just don't come back crawling here once she tramples all over your heart too busy finding one flaw about you. Don't even let her know you have a checking account at the Bank of America." Felicia is offended, incensed at the accusations thrown at her.

"You know what, *brother*; I've heard your little rants since I sat down, and nothing is coming out of your mouth but juvenile comments. As my auntie used to say, you have been 'touched in the head.' I would feel sorry for any decent, self-respecting sista who takes a chance with you. Don't you realize there are well-mannered, highly regarded Black women who appreciate and adore strong and mature Black men? It's plain to see you've been hurt by a woman in the past. Don't let that get in the way of your future. We need you." Aaron wasn't impressed with her earnest plea and continues his verbal assault at her. "Slow your roll Little Miss Muffet! Now I'm not here to disrespect you in any way but tell the truth; there are many Black women who would reject someone like me. You say you don't lower your standards, you know what you want, but tell that to the next Black woman who had her heart torn by a brother named 'Pookie,' and she goes running off to the internet claiming how evil we Black men are. So don't give me that lie about you want a good man, an intelligent man. Just be honest and say you want the wrong man. I can live with that."

"Not so." Felicia shakes her head authoritatively, swaying it from side to side. "Maybe that's good enough for all the confused women who don't know what to do with a good man once they find them, but a good Black woman like me will always seek quality. That's where my standards come from. Let's say you're right about them, shouldn't a Black woman or any woman desire a man who is willing to make them Number One in their lives? We want a man who loves God, takes care of his children, a man who makes his own money and doesn't mind spending it with the one he loves. I don't know your story Aaron, but as I said, I can tell you've been touched by someone in your past. Why are you guarding your heart with these baseless, irrational untruths? Shouldn't we Black women deserve more than that?" A small crowd gathers around Felicia, impressed with her argument. She elicits a few claps from fellow women within earshot. The fact she's a head administrator at a local medical company helps her explain her argument clearly and concisely. Daniel cringes, believing this exchange might get ugly, and listening through it all unfazed, is Aaron.

He closes his eyes for a minute, lowering his head before raising it and staring directly into hers. "You're right; I have been hurt before by a woman who didn't appreciate all the love I had for her. I took her out on dates, respected her virtue, even invited her to church, which she declined, and after all that, she wound up marrying someone else. There was no doubt I loved her! But we're the ones who approach you, and you look the other way. We're the ones who pour out our hearts, letting you how we feel, but you listen to your girlfriends who get jealous because you never had a man as good as the one you got; and you wind up leaving the good men, ending up for some dude who you don't deserve. Don't tell me a lie and say you do. We're the ones who write the poems, sing the songs, stroke your backs, sex you and down, but hear that we're boring. And according to my man, Carlos Cheatham, you Black women claim you love us, but then you cuss us

66

out something terrible when the back is turned. Therefore, I have a plan, and once that plan is complete, there better not be a Black woman running over to me to get what I have because she had her chance, and she blew it! I never forget, nor do I forgive….and that goes to all women who rejected me."

Felicia leans towards Daniel, her bulging cleavage within Aaron's eyeshot, who refuses to stare, though his eyes shift in her direction. She glances directly into Aaron's eyes, hoping he had enough sense to listen to one last plea. "Cheatham? Carlos Cheatham? That would be spoken word poet turned literary con artist? Don't you know he and all the other relationship pimps like him feel the best way to make a profit is to talk about the one thing you insecure brothers lack, confidence? If you had that, all those women who hurt you in the past would be begging to come back to you. But you rely on a chump like Cheatham so much that when you buy his books, all you do is shout up a few 'amens' when in reality, he played you. Judging by your tone of voice and the way you've addressed me so far, I can tell he's got you played like he's in a band." Felicia turns her head toward Daniel, pointing a finger in his direction. "From what I know about him, I can tell he's a good man and a prized catch for any right-thinking woman such as I. You, on the other hand, need to release that pain from your heart and stop listening to losers like Cheatham who steers you wrong or any woman who doesn't appreciate you for who you are, a Black man. Don't let him win by twisting your mind to serve his agenda. Let the universe deliver someone who can love and shows that love back. I admit we have too many on our side in this new day and age who don't appreciate the fact they are ladies, created from the side of man's rib as partners, walking hand in hand with you. That's what a mature woman needs."

Aaron steadfastly remains not impressed and unleashes another salvo in her direction. "I'm not convinced that's what you want. I think you're saying all this to fool me; make me believe all Black women are innocent when in fact, they're guilty. You read from the websites, the blogs, social media, and they all have one goal in mind; to bring us down, the Black man. You want to drag someone like me down because deep down inside, you hate me. You hate me because I'm a man, and you women are the ones who created these 'standards' because you can't control yourselves. When a sincere, truly hard-working Black man comes along, you turn him away. Don't lie because you know it's true. I can live with the rest of my life with that fact. I won't be tricked like Daniel. I know the truth, and once my plan is set in motion, I will do the same to you as you've done to me because you hate me. As God as my witness, all of you Black women truly and deeply hate me, a Black man."

Felicia refuses to send a rebuttal, knowing it was useless. The look in Aaron's eyes reveals perhaps too much to her. Instead, she turns to Daniel and asks, "How do you cope with him?"

"One day at a time." Daniel exhales a nervous breath, hoping the cannons of both sexes were out of ammo. John chuckles during the discussion adjusting his shirt underneath. Aaron believes he emerged victoriously. He thumps his chest with his fist to display the image of triumph. His celebration was short-lived however, as he feels a tap on his shoulder.

"Looks like you have nothing but strong opinions, my friend," John says.

"Hey, you have to let these women know we Black men ain't playing with them no more. I don't care what she had to say. Of course, what she said *sounds* good, except we men all know what happens in the end. I ain't the one to fall for it, though."

"Before you and that young lady were engaged in your talk, I was talking about my wife and me………"

Aaron nods, remembering the earlier conversation. "Oh yeah. So go on."

"We're trying to make another go in our relationship. You see, she and I were in love. But when that old nag of mine.........."

"Yeah, I bet she was a nag to leave you hanging like that, huh?" Aaron replies. "You know, now that I think about it, I empathize with you. I understand if your wife is a lesbian, then maybe it's better if she left with a stud, know what I mean? That's her choice, but she shouldn't leave you hanging. A man like you doesn't need a woman like that."

"Well, what do you expect when your wife's a mule?" At the mention of John's revelation, Aaron paused. Eyes opened wide.

"Hold up, come again?"

"Francesca...she's a mule. I'm married to her."

Aaron is gripped with silence that forces him to become speechless. His jaw drops. John finishes his story.

"I tell you, it doesn't matter. Women slip through your fingers like sand. I used to own this farm out in Salinas, and Francesca was a favorite of mine. We had some good times together. The parties, walks on the farm," He nudges Aaron a tad. "Nick knacking.... if you know what I mean." He winks his eye. Aaron feels sick to his stomach.

"Man, I think I'm gonna throw up."

"The farm where we lived together burned down to the ground, and for years, I've been looking for Francesca. Now I'm getting close to the end of my search." John said. Aaron mutters, "Uh-huh." nodding his head. He concludes this raggedy old man is crazy, out of his head, and out of touch with reality. Finally, with a bit of concern, Aaron questions, "Don't you have a family or doctor to go to?"

John smiles. Aaron notices the decaying yellow teeth. They were down to their last enamel. "Nope, only Francesca is my family."

Aaron is spared further punishment from the announcement his stop is next. It couldn't come soon enough. Nearing his stop, Aaron stands, excited to leave the train finally. "John, I hope you find her ass, I mean your ass...oops, your wife. I hope you find her. Seriously, I hope you find some help because I don't think you have it up here." He points a finger to his head. In an air of sarcasm, he says, "Cheer up; it could have been worse. You could have been married to a gold-digging Black woman, and you would still be homeless, ha, ha. See you too, Sista." Aaron and Daniel leave the train. Back on the railcar, Daniel's new friend Felicia while ultimately loathing Aaron, is satisfied clutching Daniel's phone number saved in her smartphone, clutched in her hand. John spots a bright orange slip lying on Aaron's seat, now empty. He squints his eyes taking a closer look at the prize. John finds out lady luck smiled on him at last.

It's one of Aaron's lottery tickets.

John raises his eyebrows, reacting in a younger voice. "Hey now, this is nice."

Later that night, Aaron buys over fifty more lottery tickets to increase his chances of victory. "Daniel, I can smell it." Aaron pumps a fist in the air, certain this is to be his night, the night all sistas should fear. The two friends are in Aaron's apartment; tickets spread out over the plush carpet. "I'm gonna win, and all of those uppity Black women will be dogged, Monroe style!" He boasts as the moment of truth, the announcement of the winning numbers neared. "Yeah, boy, I dare any stuck-up Black woman asking me to take her out to dinner, buy her an

70

expensive gift, or..." Daniel places his fingers over his lips to quiet Aaron. "Ssshh, it's starting."

As the numbers are read to the viewing audience at random, Daniel and Aaron rush to the carpet, searching for the possible winning ticket. They carefully examine the massive amount of tickets beneath them, and after an extensive half-hour search, the assumed winning slip could not be found. Aaron makes a crucial discovery amid their investigation. "Hold up; I should have two hundred and fifty lottery tickets. I counted two hundred forty-nine. Dog, where is that ticket?"

"Come on, Aaron, even if we bought the entire state of California, we can't be sure we will wind up with the winning numbers anyway." Daniel attempts to calm his friend down. Aaron stands over the carpet, wagging a finger in the air. "It's here; it has to be here!" Daniel digs his hands inside his blue jeans. "We'll just have to wait until tomorrow and find out who won." Aaron wouldn't hear of it. Instead, he keeps asking one important question while checking every single ticket.

"Where is it?"

The next morning, a restless and weary Aaron turns on the television set. News reporters found the person who won the seven hundred million. Outside an apartment complex in Canoga Park, one local female reporter holds a microphone in the face of a young Caucasian gentleman. "And your name is..."

"Todd, Todd Russell." The beaming youngster in his late twenties smiles at the camera in a long sweater and blue jeans.

"Well, Todd, you won a whopping seven hundred million with just one ticket. How do you feel and tell us what you plan to do with the big bucks?" The irritating blonde-haired field reporter speaks slightly self-centered in contrast to the clean-cut Russell's polite demeanor.

"I feel good right now, excellent. How I found the ticket was a happy accident. See, I'm one of the actors in Radically Disguised Video.com and (he waves "Hi mom!" to the camera.) yesterday I dressed up like a bum. I hopped as many different commuter buses, trains as I could. My assignment was to make up all types of stories and get people's reactions to what I said. Suddenly, this ticket appears out of nowhere, and the next thing I know, I'm a millionaire! Man, this is so freaking cool!"

"Lovely." The reporter sneers, continuing to hold her contempt and her mike. "Tell us more about your exciting adventures the day before. How did it go?"

Todd's face lights up when the camera pans in his direction. "You know, I had a great time, and it was a lot of fun. I fooled many people, including this one guy who thought I was married to a mule. Ha, ha, ha, isn't that stupid? I had the poor guy going for a minute." While Todd laughs, Aaron fumes. He is so hot he could have burned the easy chair he sits on with his thoughts. The reporter chimes in. "I understand we have a clip of what happened on that train yesterday, is that right?"

"Yes, you do." A gleeful Todd answers. Aaron's temper reaches the boiling point.   "What? They recorded everything I said? Damn!" The following clip replays the argument between Felicia and Aaron; no problem there. However, the scene that sends him spinning is the clip now showing. As Aaron is about to leave the train, he makes a few comments to 'John' with this last parting shot:

"Cheer up; it could have been worse. You could have been married to a gold-digging Black woman and you would still be homeless, ha, ha."

That comment seals his fate. No doubt there will be offended ladies interested to hear what he has to say, including his sister and three girl cousins, along with his mom, auntie, and grandma. In other words, the nightmare is only beginning. Todd continues. "If you want to watch me in action, including the encounter with that poor guy, you can watch it on Radically Disguised Video.com right......."

The microphone is yanked away from Todd's lips. The reporter shakes her head. "Sorry, we don't give advertisements for free."

Aaron helplessly watches the entire scene in front of his TV set, tempted to throw something at it. Todd was John all along. Feelings of rage erupt slowly. Aaron realizes he had been tricked, made a fool. He feels like taking a punch at Todd if he ever saw him on the street but admits it will make no difference. Watching the set again, Aaron sees the lucky Todd finish his conversation with the press.

Daniel rings the doorbell minutes later. He flashes a smile on his face while Aaron boils in anger, dressed in only a robe.

"Hey Aaron, how are you? You look dead!" Daniel is worried about his friend's appearance, not suspecting he called in sick to his job.

"Not well, you?"

I'm doing fine, but I'm sorry to know you're not feeling well. Hey, I have some news for you."

"Spill it, please."

"You remember Felicia, the young woman I spoke with on the train?"

"Yeah, what about her?" A bitter tone emerges from Aaron's lips.

"We have a date later tonight. She's driving to work in her new car." Daniel hears Felicia blow the horn below. "Gotta go. See, I told you not all Black women are the same." He departs after his last comment.

Aaron stews in the apartment alone, feeling unbelievably ill. He couldn't believe how everything changed in an instant and not for the better. His run-in with

73

Todd will be shown for all to see. His comment regarding Black women will be repeated over and over again. No doubt it will be repeated as a trending topic on social media, with millions of Black women demanding his head for his comments alone. Based on his past experiences, he will endure a living nightmare for a while. Adding insult to injury, Daniel, of all people, is going on a date with a beautiful and even Aaron has to admit, intelligent woman. Frustrated and reflecting on the events of the past day, Aaron slumps back on his sofa after learning the revelation Todd found the winning ticket, *his ticket,* and was seven hundred million dollars richer. Taking a deep sigh with a breath of resignation, Aaron rests quietly in silence with three words summarizing his view of the world this day:

"Life's a dog."

Happiness

I flash my smile wide
this love, I admit
I'm not ashamed
peace in my universe
hoping you feel the same
you do so much
I can't even begin
together in this race
called life
I know we'll win
just the two of us
holding each other's hands
I'm proud you're my baby
as I'm happy
to be called your man.

Be Yourself

These days it's all about
keeping it real
just be yourself
go your own way
on the journey
not for anyone else
only you can be the person
you dreamed of, make your plan
listen to your voice
not dissenting whispers
of both woman and man.

Be who you are
use your God-given free will
do the things
positive to the world
otherwise, you need to chill
whether you slang words
or talk very proper
it might end up
earning you dollars
just be yourself
live a full life being proud
stride with confidence
you will see
how actions speak loud.

Butterfly

A caterpillar
in a jar
spins itself
into a cocoon
turns into something wonderful
transformation
will be finished soon
finally, it emerges
out of its wrapped shell
becoming a butterfly
ready to take flight
free to soar
before it heads
into brighter light.

A simple analogy
for when our hearts grieve
when the one we hoped for
to complete our life
through no fault of their own
leave
we were wrapped in hurt
like the caterpillar
hopes were on the ground
we hid in our jar of pain
till sense came around.

We spun our cocoon

wondering why strife
is always at our door
all we want is peace
but we get drama more
hurting and hurting
furious pain inside
we weep for we aren't sure
if we dare evermore
to venture outside.

Faith triggers
from within
we know at best
we can live
that our hearts are not
toys to be played with
but gifts to others
we can give
we hold our heads up
proud to the world
battered, bruised
yet sanctified
in the hope
we wait for the day
we will be able to fly.

For all those out there
these lines I pray
touch your heart
be like the butterfly

reborn with a brand new start
this world is cold
sometimes we need
a protective cocoon
but soar like a butterfly
and hear your heart sing
a brand new tune.

Fairy Tales

Girlfriend
why are you so busy
staring at the sky?
Waiting and waiting
for that perfect guy
do you think that jolly
sticky green giant
will bend down and scoop you up
in the palm of his hand
giving you, his Thumbelina
the whole world
wanna be princess
in a dollar bill land.

Hey Sista girl
get your head off the clouds
and come inside
imaging your Aladdin
is going to treat you
to a beautiful carpet ride
you best be careful
if you give him the drama, attitude
and all that
he might be tempted to push you off
causing all your dreams
to go Splat!

Look, sweetheart

I'm not saying
you can't have fairy tales
only advising you
reality's just as good
this you should know as well
there are tons of good men
ready for your fantasy to fulfill
so don't waste another moment
letting the opportunity pass
not standing still.

So before you go off
into your own little dream world
that giant, prince, or king
might be standing next to you, girl
open your heart
explore the possibilities
that await
who knows? Maybe that king
is a cut above first-rate
let the Creator be a factor
so your spirit can say
without a doubt
you truly have a
happily ever after.

Storm Over South Central

It is another picturesque day in the city of Los Angeles, California. A warm layer of sunshine washes over the metropolis with moderate weather providing pleasant relief for the citizens huddled inside their vehicles in the middle of rush hour traffic on busy freeways or surface streets. A multitude of users travels along with a daily transit system that takes them to their points of destination through the Southland. Tourists from different parts of the globe enjoy the glamour of Hollywood; alluring filters of sand attract individuals who frequent the beaches. Young and old thrill seekers indulge in the adventure of amusement parks. Recreation parks set the stage for family reunions, lovers cherish moments of togetherness on a secret outing, and friends wherever they gather to enjoy good times. All is at rest in the big city. All is at peace on a day in the endless summer for which this region is known for. The postcards and reality shows reveal the truth of the Los Angeles they've heard about.

This is only part of the story which is told, but it is all but a lie.

Deep in the heart of the Southside where the quality of life differs greatly for those citizens residing in a "war zone." A day does not go by where fierce popping sounds of high-powered machine guns are heard within earshot. Drugs sold consistently on street corners from ambitious young people unaware while they sought to get ahead, morally pollute the very neighborhoods in which they live. Paramedics sorrowfully throw yet another white sheet over an unfortunate victim whose blood spills on the mean streets of this grief-stricken community. Long-time residents accustomed to the violence can be heard raising their whispered prayers to heaven; when will it stop? When will it end? Some wondered if the senseless killings would ever cease. Few figured the carnage would end when God decides in His divine wisdom and time of His choosing the sun has set on its final day. In either case, there is nothing that could be done in the minds of the sorrowful residents. Nothing.

One day, an unusual massive scarlet cloud hovers ominously over the vast region of South Central Los Angeles. Youngsters riding their bikes on a sidewalk sprawled with graffiti stop to glance at the huge red haze hovering above them covering several miles. A single mother in a housing project in the Central Alameda district hangs her children's garments on a clothesline. She takes a brief pause from her chores, glaring at the sky. Members of a neighborhood street gang huddling on a street corner spew profanity when the sun vanishes from sight. The gigantic cloud is accompanied by a harsh but steady wind, blowing fiercely throughout the inner city. Thunder and lightning roar deep within. A barber closing his shop after another long business day looks at the troubled heavens, and mentions to a colleague, "You know, it looks like it might rain."

The sky grows even darker. The wind continues to blow but feels much colder, unrelenting. Lightning and thunder booms louder, bursting the eardrums of the mortals below. Then it falls, the rain. A heavy drizzle pours down, sending most people scrambling for shelter. This deluge feels different, unique from any other shower ever known.

It rains blood.

It must have been quite a surprise to most witnessing the uncanny crimson liquid fall on the streets. A mailman on his route stands astonished as an envelope he delivers

83

changes from pure white to a wet saturated shade of red. A tall young Black man returning home from a nearby junior college discovers ruby red stains on his yellow Lakers jacket. Besides the distinctive color, the red storm has another surprise for individuals trapped in the middle of it; the unmistakable odor of death. As the rain hits the ground, the unpleasant smell rises high in the air causing the residents to go inside and lock their doors. There would be no reason to step outside.

On the porch of a residential home, a young child sits with his elderly grandmother. Her decaying physical body houses a sharp mind within experienced to know the ways of Man and his many flaws. With her wrinkled hands, she pulls a scarf over her hair, showing its age. Gently, the frail woman of a dark skin shade tucks in her sweater, keeping her warm from the bitter cold. Lifting her head up as far as her ancient eyes could see, the grandmother mutters a few words under her breath. Her small grandson asks her, "Nana, it's raining red. What does that mean?" The grandmother turns her head, stares at her grandchild with weary eyes in a mixture of remorse and shame. She cannot articulate the words to tell her young kin about the unusual phenomenon they find themselves in. He is too young to comprehend, too innocent to understand the ways of the world fully. This knowledge hurts her deep, for she knows as he grows into an older, mature adult, his pure heart might be tainted in a world that is not quite as pure. She cannot explain to him her thoughts of the crimson rain falling on them with its putrid smell. The grandmother believes a deeper religious meaning from the heavens is being enacted to learn and to fear. Reaching over to her grandson, she wraps her loving arms around the boy, kissing him on the forehead. With quivering lips and a solemn tone replies, "These are our days of reckoning, baby."

Days of reckoning. Three words that strike fear in her heart, more so than anything else. The storm of blood is just another circumstance created out of fear. She recognizes others who didn't live under the conditions she endures are unfamiliar and ignorant of this four-letter word that carries much power. Fear to walk the streets at night or in modern times, daylight. Fear to go by the nearby store lest residents could be robbed, beaten, or killed. Fear to wear certain colors in specific neighborhoods where legions of gangs dominate, becoming another statistic for being at the wrong place at the wrong time. Yes, the emotion of fear grips many over time, its power growing day after day. Black and brown youngsters sit in their living rooms afraid to venture outside, terrified of the droplets of blood falling upon them, the tortuous odor surrounding them. A ten-year-old girl viewing the dark ruby red precipitation wonders if she'll ever see the sun again. No one leaves their homes becoming de facto prisoners trapped within, a condition they were used to under 'normal' circumstances. Other residents tried in vain to resume their *normal* lives but to no avail. Vehicle drivers braving a trip through the crimson storm are hindered, frustrated by the messy red smear forming on their windshields; local transit buses and rail lines cancel their routes passing through the areas affected by the storm. A few citizens find moving from the community a viable answer to their dilemma. Not all could take the same approach, for they have nowhere to move to and not enough financial resources to act upon.

A week passes since the storm of blood first appeared. Even as gang violence decreases and drug dealing subsides, the tremendous dark cloud expands in horrifying length, moving Eastward to cities such as Huntington and Walnut Park. In a fascinating quirk of irony, the storm did not appear in the city's more affluent neighborhoods on the

Westside or even downtown, leaving speculation by those affected why their wealthier counterparts are not touched. Accusations of governmental control of the weather are raised, along with elaborate conspiracy theories and other hysterical claims born of tongues and the internet.

The storm of blood catches the attention of local law enforcement. Noticing the steep drops in drive-bys and murders associated with street violence, a legion of squad cars from municipalities and districts on the outer edge of the storm were parked just outside the gigantic cloud covering nearly all of the boundaries; Willowbrook to the south, Watts to Central Alameda to the east, Historic South-Central to West Adams to the north, and Baldwin Hills-Crenshaw to Crenshaw-Manchester on the West. The residents of Baldwin Hills-Crenshaw were incensed yet questioned out loud why their area is affected by the storm. Police officers step out of their vehicles, snap pictures of the massive, intimidating cloud, and even offer a word of thanks in prayer.

A Latina in her forties living on the East side of the city cries to her husband in the safe confines of their kitchen, "Why us? Please tell me, why us?" Like many before him, the husband shakes his head unable to find a suitable answer for the unanswerable. Churches within the crimson storm were packed, full to capacity. Every service was crowded with faithful and new churchgoers, including Sunday evenings. Disheartened worshipers show up in desperation to save their souls from damnation believing the storm of blood is a sign of a much larger, eternal punishment. Preachers plead with their followers to pray to God with faith the storm will abate. Choirs sang inspired spiritual songs amid much crying behind the pews by many in attendance requesting an explanation why the scarlet shower has arrived. The big question is uttered from so

86

many lips. "Is this a punishment from God?" and the inevitable response, "If so, why?"

Political leaders were silent if not humbled, intensely concerned at the bizarre occurrence which appeared first in South Central and now threatens to spread into other communities, the populations they represent. Their mouths truly declared they had nothing planned to help the citizens in the middle of the storm. What relief could they provide? The issue involving the rain wasn't a question of money or use of police or promised public programs, but a question. An enigma those in the political arena could not answer with tricky words or tough talk saved for an election year. Perhaps it should be preserved as a mystery, a difficult challenge to answer.

Reports from local and national cable news programs featured the storm diligently. Stark images were posted on the front cover of magazines and increased traffic flow on the internet. Videos filmed within the storm by YouTube users shared their experiences with an unknown multitude of perhaps billions watching each updated detail, breathtaking and tragic at the same time. Students who tried to resume their college lives in junior college and major universities like USC found how foolhardy it was to enter their classes with blood-soaked backpacks, a disgusting taste in the foods they ate, and their drinks ingested. Other ripple effects of the storm caused gardens to spoil, and plants were dying, not fed with adequate water needed to survive. The Rose Garden in Exposition Park and adjacent Coliseum turned flowing green grass into puddles of crimson.

Various news media outlets sent brave reporters to cover the storm to give the interested audience a view of the unique and tragic phenomenon in South Central. A female field reporter in a raincoat speaks in front of a camera, recording her very words, emotions of what she

87

stood in the middle of. Her face contorts in repulsion, watching droplets of red splash upon her jacket, even her hair as it seeps through the baseball cap she wore. "I'm standing right here in the middle of this storm in Exposition Park, and I have to tell you, it's unlike anything I've ever seen here. This odor is......unbearable. I do not lie. It smells as if a thousand people have been left for dead, left on the streets to rot." She holds a bloody rose in her hand. "As you can see in my hand, a rose has withered and died, a result of the lack of vegetation and greenery surrounding me. Our meteorologists in the past few weeks have been unable to determine when this storm appeared and when it will leave. Who knows when this will stop? My guess is no one knows."

Comments from the reporter's mouth revive past and perhaps present fears of what South Central used to be. A history no one wants to repeat as the city is in the middle of a transformation of new high-rise buildings and blocks upon blocks of what leaders call "affordable housing" for long time low-income residents although they will make way for new neighbors of a different and affluent ethnicity moving in. Now that the storm has appeared in full force, the old fears resurface under a frightening and dark representation of what occurred before. These fears were the engines for news bureaus across the country to direct their news coverage of the storm. World affairs and national politics would have to take a back seat for once.

News cable talk shows across both city and country and on the internet made the storm a national curiosity. Newspapers print special reports almost daily. Guests, so-called "experts," discuss the strange phenomenon in the area. Inside a studio originating from New York, a remote is set up by a conservative-leaning cable news network to interview a woman whose home is in the middle of the storm.

The bombastic veteran host of over thirty years of experience sits behind his desk espousing his opinions of what this all means with the feeling his viewership made of elderly men and women aligned with his views will agree.

"South Central Los Angeles....excuse me, South Los Angeles," He speaks mockingly, "is a community known for its deadly drive-bys, ravenous thugs, street gangs, and its endless supply of sex, drugs, and death is being deluged right now by a powerful storm....of blood. Just how powerful? Well, you haven't heard of any killings in the area recently, have you? What we see right now is a mandate from the Almighty Himself to citizens of that community to get their houses in order before it's too late. We have with us right now a Miss Violet Johnson. She is thirty-four years of age, a single mother of two children. She lost a son to a walk-by shooting at school last year. She lives in the heart of this treacherous tempest, and she's agreed to speak with us tonight." The host raises his hand as the camera quickly captures the image of the frail build of Violet silently sitting in her chair with a determined stare on her face.

"Miss Johnson, Violet, can you hear me? This is Peter Flannery in New York. How are you this evening?"

"Fine, and you?" She spoke methodically and directly to the camera.

"I am well, thank you. I have to ask Violet, how do you handle something like this? How do you cope?"

"Just as I've always have Mr. Flannery, one day at a time."

"You know, I've had a meeting with staff, and we're not aware of how this storm came about. Scientists and preachers are baffled about the meaning and significance of such an occurrence. Violet, what do you make of it?"

"Mr. Flannery," Violet leans forward in her chair. Her eyes visible enough to penetrate the viewers at home, making sure they listen to what she is about to say. "I was born and raised here in South Central Los Angeles. They may call it South Los Angeles, SOLA, or some other junk like that, but it's still South Central to me. I've heard you earlier, and I want your viewers to know I'm a hard-working mother who only wants to provide a better life for my children."

Flannery interrupts. "Admirable Violet, but no one wants to......."

"LISTEN!" Violet shouts. "You asked me to be on your show. If you *listen*, I'll have an answer to your question, so you're so inclined to one." She continues, more deliberate than before with her words. "You've mentioned the past history of what South Central used to be, and I'm not surprised in the least that's what you or your viewers think. In all of this Mr. Flannery, everyone forgot about us. Everyone forgot about the ones who lived and died here wanting to have a peaceful life. It's like we weren't accepted by society but thrown away. I thought I could be strong and live through my baby's death and encourage my other children to keep going strong." Remorseful tears fell from her eyes.
"Now.........now..........my baby's gone, and my hopes rest on my other children. I wanted my baby to graduate from high school. She was only a few days away, and she was so close.........." Violet pauses for a moment holding back the painful tears anxious to burst out, emotions set to explode.

Flannery's audience hung on Violet's every word. "I ask all of you out there watching me, seeing this rainfall every day; it's just another thing we have to deal with. We can deal with the police brutality, businesses refusing to build on land they own, all of that, that's what we've always dealt with. I know you all wanted to hear about this storm. That's all you and your viewers care about, Mr. Flannery, so let me tell you. As far as this rain keeps

90

pouring down, and I don't know if God the Father is doing this or not, I know this. All of you who aren't facing this, be glad. Enjoy your normal lives because what is happening to us now certainly can happen to you. This storm could have shown up almost anywhere, but it settled here in my neighborhood, that's all. I thought after the gangs were off the streets and the drug selling stopped, this storm would fade away. Now I'm not so sure if it ever will. I'm...I'm sorry. I can't say no more." Cutting Violet's feed, Flannery responds to her impassioned speech.

"Violet, I deeply sympathize with your loss; I truly do. That, however, does not explain why this rain of blood has materialized in your community. Who knows what will happen next? I'm not sure, are you? All I can say, Violet and our millions of viewers at home, is that although you didn't deserve it, it's about damn time some justice is being administered even if it's divine, allegedly. For continuing coverage of this storm and further developments, stay tuned to the National Update for all breaking news." Flannery notices the dismayed reactions from his producers for not showing much empathy to Violet at all with a slight glance to the side. Indifferent to their feelings, Flannery addresses his audience by looking straight at the camera directed towards him. "We'll be right back."

Another two weeks pass. The red cloud expands across the county landscape to communities in the San Fernando Valley to the Inland Empire, the Westside to Orange County. Dwellers of these areas were shocked in absolute astonishment to watch the red storm appear in their vicinity, raising their fists in outrage and anger. The blood-soaked rainfall lands on their driveways, expensive cars, ruining the sparkling shining paint on them. Now the affluent voices and others long unaffected began to shout.

"Why? Why? It's not fair!" Not fair indeed. Perhaps the storm grew to educate these individuals how it felt to be

91

afraid like their fellow men and women in the metropolis. Maybe it is a sign to those who thought they would be untouched to not take things for granted. It also showed they are not immune as well. So many questions were raised about the storm, and its arrival didn't matter now. It had arrived, and it was spreading.

Within a month, the storm enlarges, blanketing the state of California. The glamour of Hollywood, the majesty of the Golden gate bridge vanish. Orange crops and produce are spoiled. California's economy, the sixth-largest in the world, faces the perilous danger of grinding to a halt. Beaches colored with the red stains of blood upon the sands and in the tidewater, did not look romantic at all.

The red cloud continues to expand in monstrous circumference. It floats ominously over the Western states of Oregon, Nevada, and Arizona. Then it reaches Utah, Texas, and the Midwest. Choruses of shouts ring throughout the land, the 'righteous' lift up their hands in protest.

"Why? Why us? What have we done wrong?"

The storm threatens to smother the entire country in blood. It was too late to stop it; it has grown and shows signs of not stopping its treacherous path. To note, the storm appears at a cross burning in the South, dousing the flames of hate. It rains in Chicago during a neo-Nazi march. Even skinheads pause with fear unknown to them as the rain falls on their clothes. It floats overhead in the state of Florida, where outside a courtroom, a gentleman triumphantly celebrates his acquittal of allegedly shooting an unarmed teenager who plans to drive in the rain, only to witness his vehicle drenched. The foul odor of death causes his celebration to end prematurely. It falls with a tremendous downpour in Ferguson, Missouri, where a member of law enforcement ended a young man's life. Anywhere and everywhere, bigotry, class disputes, even wanton violence such as brutality reared, the storm appears. Once more, questions continued to flow by an unsuspecting and fearful multitude about the source of the raindrops. It made no difference now, nor did it matter. The United States of America is slowly engulfed in a gigantic, massive cloud raining blood from California to New York, North Dakota to Texas.

One wonders if this tragic phenomenon has become what the grandmother revealed to her grandson on that same porch in South Central, watching the blood-filled sky.

These are our days of reckoning, baby.

And the storm continues to grow.

I Cannot

I cannot
be the person
you request of me
I'm unable to spend millions
transporting us
to different countries
it is not within my power
to give you that house
you want on the hill
I'm only an individual
who can love you
with all his will.

I cannot
fulfill your each and every
passionate desires
I can, however
offer solace
when you're frustrated and tired
yet I cannot
agree on everything
you have to say
I'm just one man
cognitive spirit
a piece of divine clay.

Therefore

I shall do my best
limited though I may be
to share the profit in my soul
in the hopes
our investment will grow
there are things I can cater to
give a chance, take a shot
but don't expect me to change outside
the person I am
to that request, indeed I cannot.

A Black Poem

Every man of color
under the sound
of this voice
today in this
brave new dawn
we're faced with a choice
to maintain an image
that becomes our reality
or break that mindset
with some factuality.

For so long
my sole purpose
according to
the dominant society
is to play ball and entertain
but it never occurred to them
I might leave something
on the brain
but when you're perceived
as being an educational reject
I understand the shock
when I show
I also have intellect.

Let's understand this:
Man calls me nigger
the Lord calls me blessed

evil words residing in the hearts of men
but they too shall be put to rest
Man crucified the Son of The Creator
because He spoke the truth
he'll do the same
to anyone who dares
offer proof.

We speak of kingdoms of the past
experts can surely convey
but let's go over
the dark facts of American history
Washington, DeBois
Carver and Woodson
even Bunche and Drew
I didn't see a thug
in the talented group
you agree with that, don't you?
Douglass, Attucks
Meredith, Robinson
and the man we know
as X
he, along with Dr. King
challenged our consciousness
pushing equality and respect
but there are more examples
other men of color
who taught us to live
as common men
not limited to sisters

and brothers.

As long as we live
we'll always deal
with things not proper and right
but we continue to see the day
when we say to those myths and lies
"Leave! Disappear! Get out of our sight!"

Just Another Loneliness Poem

Loneliness
the bitter pill
settling in my heart
emotional discomfort
rumbling still
for days, hours
long, disturbing years
I've seen my joys
turn into bitter tears.

A wrathful demon
harbored deep
in my soul
ordered to destroy
my mind, body
essential flow
convincing me all
self-negativity
is justified and right
sapping my strength
diminishing my fight.

Loneliness
it takes a while
to recover
when you find good people
and supportive lover
yet it strikes at quiet times

like a tall mountain
it must be defeated
though it's a hard climb
it is all worth it
even when your energy is drained
a smile will form
when victory is attained.

I'm A Black Man

I'm a Black man
strong in number
with a sound mind
do you hear the thunder?
I guess you can't
since you're so busy
putting men down
you can keep me underwater
but I surely won't drown
that's right, sister girl
correct girlfriend
think you can break my back?
Please, all you can do is bend.

I'm one of the chosen
part of the elite few
who shouldn't waste time
dealing with the venom
you casually spew
I have to go forth
make my path
because when I opened up
my heart to you
about my aspirations
you started to laugh
when I do make it
and I most certainly will
I wonder

101

how you're going to face me
with indifferent smile
or guilty chill?

Now, these hip cats
imitate my slang
but a noose
they will never find
cause they ain't
the one's society wants to hang
shucking and jiving
thinking acting Black is cool
wait until they find out
the color wasn't in style
in Jim Crow days
racist old school.

I even have different girls
yearning to be my fans
but I'm down with the sistas
for I'm a Black man
but if you don't back me
explore what I'm all about
then believe this
there's nothing to you I can sell
because you're the one
who'll bailout?

Why did I say that?
you wouldn't lend me your support

obviously in your heart
you thought I was someone else
always coming up short
let me tell you
you're not worthy
of putting out my fire
if you refuse to give me love
then ambition shall be
my greatest desire.

So go ahead, sista
roll your eyes
to the back of your neck
too bad you don't want
to see your mistake
of the man
you'd happen to reject
if only, only
you taken the time to see
that I am
a real Black man
given a chance
who will always
be at your side, guaranteed.

The Albatross

For Denton Rudolph, it is another in a long string of sleepless nights. There is no doubt the recently widowed gentleman tosses and turns relentlessly on his living room couch. He is irritated and restless in the small confines of his South Los Angeles apartment in the Baldwin Hills district. In vain, he attempts to lie gently even though he is troubled with painful memories flooding his mind. His eyes ascend towards the peach-covered wall opposite the foot of his couch. There rests a painting of refreshing blue icy sea waves in the background. The foreground stands a white feathered, orange beaked, web-footed bird on the tan-colored beach, an albatross.

Denton doesn't turn his eyes away from the painting. It was a gift from his deceased wife, who made her final journey eight months earlier. The more he glances at the painting, the more heartbreak tears his soul open, forcing him to take action. He can no longer endure the gripping, solemn loneliness surrounding him. He walks to his closet, pulling out a windbreaker jacket, slipping it around his medium broad shoulders, down to his athletically toned build. Glancing at the mirror, Denton brushes the strands of his low fade haircut. The young Black man under thirty years of age ties his sneaker shoestrings before exiting out the door. Quickly Denton places his keys in his jacket pocket and descends downstairs, pounding the wooden staircase with his shoes. He makes his way from the cold chilly apartment building to the even harder outside world. He tugs his jacket as he faces the rays of the slowly rising morning sun creeping slowly from the East.

At the same time each morning, Denton strolls down Marlton Avenue. It gives him a chance to clear his mind, to not think of the loss of his wife, Levitica. Passing through the row of apartment houses on either side with neighbors or visitors rushing to get inside their parked cars, his eyes catch a slight view of the downtown L.A. skyline with lights flickering off the skyscrapers he observes. Walking further down Marlton, Denton witnesses the Cudahy-West Hollywood Metro line bus turning Westward on Santa Rosalia Drive. He knows of a driver who often passes through quoting biblical scriptures that puts him in a calm mood for the rest of his day.

As he stands on the corner of Marlton and Santa Rosalia near the YMCA where he spent his days as a youth, Denton shrugs his shoulders of the latest development, a new hospital in the old Marlton Square property and other future construction projects underway not meant for his kind, but for the new neighbors moving in such as the fiftyish Caucasian woman in a jogging suit with short grey hair walking a couple of dogs in his direction. A couple of awkward brief "hellos" are said before the woman passes him by. Her German Shepherds' tails sway back and forth as they walk along the edges of the front lawns of houses they approach. Denton feels as if the world changed around him in an instant. Even passing through the Baldwin Hills-Crenshaw Plaza, where Denton frequents often, is in the midst of a transformation promising to change its look entirely to a 'town square' format shopping complex it has been recognized for. He treads the same streets he carefully protected himself from gangs; now is home to a different unit, one with other ethnicities and outlook on life. Something in the morning breeze reminds Denton of a choice he's debated for a while. *Should I sell it or not?*

He asks the question in his mind over what to do with his late wife's painting. "If I sell it, Levitica's death won't hurt me as much, or maybe it could cause me to miss her more if I do?" It is a decision Denton has to act on in the future. This is on his mind as he crosses the street on his way toward Martin Luther King Junior Boulevard. One he didn't want to explore further but understands he may be forced to do so soon.

Gazing at the time on his cell phone, Denton notices the time is fifteen minutes past six. He walks a few more blocks to the corner of Crenshaw and King, past the ongoing development of a new Metro rail line down Crenshaw to the south. He walks past a crowd of passengers waiting for the Metro South Bay Galleria to Downtown L.A. bus line at the front of a renovated neighborhood diner called the Revolution Cafe that Denton visits on most days. As he takes a seat near the front entrance, Denton gazes to the other side of the café spotting a few Black men and one Caucasian huddle near one of the long tables. It isn't unusual to see one or two, perhaps ten people inside buying breakfast or a cup of coffee to start their day at this time of the morning. What makes this crowd different than the usual is that it has a group of construction workers finishing an all-night shift. Their presence reminds Denton of his time working for a corporation in the city as an architect supervising a new theater in the downtown area. Due to Levitica's passing and the project completed shortly after that, he was released from his job, now left with a severance package until he finds another place of employment.

Denton sits in his chair, taking small sips. He doesn't feel rushed to finish his drink; instead, he observes with his eyes the men sitting in a booth across from him. Lowering his head, Denton hears with curiosity of the discussion taking place between them. He feels engaged as an observer than a participant. Quietly, he pays attention to what they had to say.

"Plain, did you know that woman on Bronson Avenue sold her house a few days ago?" These are the words of an older man with a caramel complexion dressed casually in a button-down sweater and slacks. Using his two hands to lift a stack of dominoes from the wooden table, his eyes glance at a man with a darker complexion also dressed casually in a similar outfit. He wears a fedora on his head, nods to signal a response to what he listened to. Denton recognizes him as one of the 'wise elders' of the neighborhood. He is known as Isaiah Benjamin Plain or I.B. Plain for short. Every morning at the same time, he and his best friend Eugene gather with a few domino-playing partners, both young and old, for a friendly round of games in the booth.

"Better watch that three-five in your hand." Lenora is the gray-haired woman sitting on the other side of the booth. She isn't very tall, with a height slightly over five feet. Years added girth to what used to be a very shapely and attractive body. She is the most accomplished player in the group and possesses a sharp tongue, always aware of what set of dominoes her opponents hold in their hands. Eugene glances over to the young man sitting next to him, taking notice of the nervous hand, struggling to place the correct ivory piece on the table, the one Lenora quickly surmises. "Don't be scared of her youngster. Study long, study wrong."

"I'm cool with it." The young man extends a long arm across the table, laying his domino flat. As the game continues, Plain answers Eugene's question regarding the old house. "Yeah, I knew about it. The fifth home sold this month."

"Guess there ain't no stopping these white folks now," Lenora says pointedly. "Look what's happening across the street with the mall. They're tearing that down and building a hotel on the other side."

"Just the other day, I met some white folks inside that new hospital on Santa Rosalia," Eugene recalls, laying his piece on the table. "Didn't talk much. I guess they were

107

there for a checkup. This whole thing, what you young people call it? Gentrify……"

"Gentrification." The young man interjects. "All started with that new rail line they are building on Crenshaw. It changed Leimert Park, and it's doing the same in this neighborhood." The elders focus on the youth's comments. He appears to be knowledgeable wearing Jamaican apparel. His hair twists into dreadlocks; his brown eyes are so wide and bright, the elders feel his powerful gaze as he stares at them. "When those white people finish moving here, there won't be a conscious physical community left. You notice what they did to West Oakland, right? You know the same thing is happening with Leimert and even here. We're being erased."

"So what solutions, if any, do you have?" Plain taps him on the shoulder. "I know of one; don't sell your home if you can afford the cost. I remember a movie my grandson and I watched that stressed the very same thing."

"Mr. Plain, I see you've watched Boyz N The Hood." The young man nods. "Yes, the character Furious Styles warned us this would happen. While people enjoyed the same actor in his role of Morpheus in a different movie asking the character Neo to choose either a blue or red pill, Furious told us not to accept any pill that will cause us to fall asleep and lose our focus."

"Wise words, young man. White folks love to talk about their matrix. We're over here trying to survive in the real world." Finished with their first round, Lenora sends her compliments and social critique towards him as she shuffles the dominoes. "Let me tell you this. The landlords raise the rent, which makes it difficult for people like me to stay in my apartment. You know why they're doing it. But Plain wants a solution, so I would love to hear what you have to say."

The young man leans back, straightening his shoulders. Denton glances at him, offering what solutions are needed. He decides it's best to focus on finishing his cup. He believes the answers to the discussion he overheard are best left for another day. Another waitress waves hello to him, taking his order scribbling it on her pad now that his stomach desires breakfast. His younger brother Edwin, a security guard on a rare day off, walks through the front entrance and waves to the patrons inside. He sits near his brother, joining him. Edwin has a firm muscular build, standing a tad above six feet tall. He towers over his brother by at least three inches. His skin color is a shade lighter than his sibling's. "What up, Denton? How are you feeling today?"

"The same." Denton takes a sip, images of Levitica flood his mind. His tired eyes stare soberly at the table. "Thinking about it, aren't you?" Edwin replies.

"Yeah, yeah, I am." Denton shifts his thoughts, focusing on the painting. "Decision's so damn hard; I haven't slept in days."

"It's best if you sell it. My girl agrees that you should do that. After all, it's a great deal. The interested guy said it's good and would be one of his featured works in his gallery."

"I'm not worried about the deal. I'm just concerned about what happens after." Denton clasps his hands over his head, trying to hold back the hurt that has been inside him for so long. He pauses. "Who knows? I might not sell it after all."

Edwin's face changes, showing disappointment. "What do you mean? After all I've done for you? You're going to pull back on the offer? I understand how much it means to you and all, but you would be crazy not to take the money! I know you're smarter than that."

"Look, Edwin," Denton leans forward. "Don't push me!"

"Don't be a scared little boy like you've been all your life." Edwin retorts.

"And you do nothing but get young girls pregnant and run off!"

"Damn you!" Edwin is incensed. "Go to hell!"

"If I do, it won't be long before you join me!" Both men hold clinched fists next to their sides, a sign of raised hostilities but not much else. They cool their passions for a moment as not to draw attention to the patrons around them. Denton smacks his lips and whispers, "Fine. Just push me, that's all."

The eyes of the two brothers are locked in anger. Fists remain clenched. Hearts pound rapidly with quiet rage. In a huff, Denton jumps out of his seat, storming out of the cafe. Plain looks in Edwin's direction with a raised hand containing a domino. "Is everything okay over there? What happened to the man who was with you?" Edwin shrugs his shoulders. He looks around the café and, with a deep breath, explains, "Nothing, just family business."

The time approaches nine o'clock. The rays of bright sunshine keep rising high in the sky; the full effects of the sun's rays won't occur for another hour or so.

Denton retreats to his apartment. This time, the walk doesn't absolve the anger he feels for Edwin; burying his head in his pillow doesn't take that away. Laying in his bed for a minute, he allows silence to take over the room, cooled by the sounds of the air conditioner he didn't shut down on his earlier departure for his daily walk. The rumbling in his body reminds the lonely widower he forgot his breakfast, now paying the price of an empty stomach. It wasn't the only thing in his life that is empty. Laying on his bed, Denton reaches to the other side, expecting the warmth of a female form next to him, only to find nothingness. An

110

overflow of tears fills his eyes as his eyelids slowly close. The long walk back made him sleepy, extremely tired. He struggles to stay awake but does not fight the feeling overwhelming him to rest. His eyes gradually shut, sending Denton to drift into the dark realm of sleep.......

He first met his future wife on a college campus in Texas, not far from Corpus Christi. They shared the same African American history class. Levitica regularly sat in the front row, a remarkable "A" student, while Denton admired her from afar in the third row, maintaining a modest "C" average. The first time she captured his total attention was when this beautiful woman wore a dark-colored blouse with a matching skirt in the quad area. He taps one of his friends, a six-foot-three muscular Black man wearing a buttoned shirt noticing Levitica laughing and joking with friends within eyesight.

"It's that girl from class!"

"Who?" His friend asked, staring in Levitica's direction.

"Her! LaTisha, LaVeronica......."

"Oh, you mean Levitica?" His friend turned towards Denton with a puzzled look for mispronouncing her name. "She's nice. You like her?"

"Yeah, I do. What do you think? You think she likes me too?"

"I don't know." His friend scratches his head, continuing to stare at Levitica's bright smile and carefree attitude. "That's up to you. Maybe if you ask her...."

"Dude, I got you. I have to be the one to approach her. Man, she's so fine. I have to get with her."

"Don't wait until you're an old man."

It wasn't hard to figure out why Denton was attracted to Levitica. His eyes were fixated on the voluptuous black woman dressed with exaggerated sensual curves, sparkling

111

light brown eyes, long flowing braided hair covering most of her back and part of her behind. Although she was a joy to see and his attraction for her grew each moment, it was sealed with a soft, genteel voice which had a bit of the country in it but pleasant to hear. An intelligent mind guided her body, and her friendly, witty attitude fleshed out the persona of the woman who captured Denton's soul. When class ended, Denton ventured to the campus eatery. That's where Levitica would be. Every time he found her, she would sit with friends at a nearby table, cursing at himself when he passed up chances to speak with her. One day after class ended, she sat alone. Thinking all or nothing, he courageously pulled a chair next to her. Levitica briefly glanced in his direction and smiled. Confidence waning, Denton prepared to leave from her sight.

His nerves almost exploded. He couldn't believe this sensual beauty took a liking to him when based on her body structure, she could have any man she desired. Standing at five foot seven, Levitica was not an amazon but possessed a fine body and mind. She was desirable to him, friendly with a warm smile. He had to know more about her.

"Hey," she spoke with a womanly tone accompanied by her country accent. He froze, expecting a quiet rejection. "Where are you going? Come, sit next to me." She patted her hand on the chair, urging his return.

The nervous suitor was surprised at the request. "You sure?"

"Yes, I'm sure." She mentioned in a tender, sweet voice.

Denton sat down and edged even closer to her. Levitica could see his hands shaking. She gently placed a calm hand over his exposed right palm. She lightly grasped it, continuing to smile. Denton mustered some courage and

112

inquired, "What happened to your friends? Aren't they usually with you at this time?"

Levitica laughed politely. "No. They all have finals. I'm glad too. Now I have a chance to talk with you."

"Yes, you do, and I thank you for the opportunity."

"You're welcome. Let me share a secret; I've always noticed you." She admitted. Denton was shocked. "You look so intelligent, and you have your head on straight. I mean, you're a good guy. I'm impressed, but I seem to have a hard time getting to know you. Why do you run away whenever I'm here? I won't bite, honest."

"Levitica, it's not that." Denton confessed, "I was afraid you wouldn't like me, I guess. You see, I don't know anyone here, but when I saw you, I liked you. I like your beauty, your brains, everything about you. I just wanted you to be a friend and perhaps.........more than that." She smiled, touching him with her other hand.

"I'm so glad you told me." A sense of relief rushed all over Levitica, playfully holding her chest. "May I ask you a question?"

"Sure."

"May I be your friend?"

"Yes."

A blossoming relationship had begun.

During their conversations, Denton discovered a few facts about her. She had no real family to speak of. Her father, a prominent religious preacher in the small Texas town she was raised in, was beaten and killed in a racial crime when she was five; her mother died of cancer when she turned ten. Her aunt, who lived in San Antonio, took custody of Levitica until she started college. To satisfy Denton's questions about her name, Levitica mentions it's from Leviticus. Since her father was a preacher, he decided to name a child after reading the books from the bible. Denton didn't care about the name, but it gave him a reason

113

to explain it to his friends back home in California when he faced questions about the lovely young woman he met.

In Levitica's case, she enjoyed Denton's company. It was much better when she overheard a rude comment by a classmate, one she regretted listening to.

"Damn! Do you know Levitica, that chesty girl in African American Studies class? She's got some serious sweater meat! I know her man must suck on them every night!" She heard the pointed jeers of a fellow student laughing out loud to his friends down the hallway surrounding him as he shares his lust for her. Within earshot, she heard his comments, and they stung her deep. She knew her figure was outrageously curvaceous, but it was something she had no control over, although she adored her figure and decided not to reduce or alter a single body part to silence her lustful admirers. Her father once drove her to a doctor who suggested breast reduction, yet once Levitica heard each detail of the procedure, she told her father she didn't want to go through with it. Her back, already firm, could handle the extra weight up top, and as long as she kept a healthy shape, the extra weight on her chest wouldn't be a burden.

She spent a lifetime hearing comments from men in public, primarily rude and crass. Levitica wasn't the one to engage in social media. She was afraid to post a picture of herself due to women's treatment on the internet by lewd, horny men who she felt would drive themselves crazy once they saw her figure online. Believing it wasn't worth the hassle and stress, Levitica allowed Denton to surf the internet on her behalf, posting pictures of them that displayed only a smile, shots above her chest, or both. Denton was the first man she ever knew who treated her with respect, a man she could enjoy being herself around, a person who accepted her as she was, not as a fantasy object.

114

The young couple had become good friends. They went to movies, had dinners, and studied together. Their relationship developed slowly. Within a year, they decided to become romantic mates. By the end of their senior year, they were engaged. At the university, Denton and Levitica concentrated on their majors. It was Business for her, Architecture for him.

Before their wedding, Denton had an important announcement for her. They met in Levitica's small yet cozy dorm room. The couple sat on the couch during their usual pastime, watching movies. Levitica could tell Denton looked worried during their movie watching. She was concerned over what seemed to bother him. There was a pause where he had a chance to explain what was on his mind.

"My uncle called from California today. He knows a construction contractor personally informed him he needed someone; experience not a real factor to help this contractor plan out a project for an office building in the downtown Los Angeles area. My uncle convinced him I was qualified, and the contractor agreed to have me on his staff."

"When are you expected to show up?" Levitica asked.

"I have to report to him right after graduation. It is in California, and I didn't know if you wanted to come with me. If you don't, we will work it out somehow." Levitica giggles. "You don't have to worry about that, Denton. I wouldn't mind following you. I've been anxious to see what California looks like, the movie stars, the lifestyle, all of that." She assured him, rubbing his head gently. Her decision was final. Soon thereafter, Levitica quit her job in her friend's beauty salon in town and arranged to have her belongings packed and sent to California preparing for her big day, which was her wedding.

The wedding ceremony was memorable. It took place in a small local church Levitica's aunt attended. Bridesmaids wore stunning velvet outfits and groomsmen shined in their white tuxedos. Levitica shook like a leaf. Denton took deep nervous breaths. This was a significant step in their lives, one they wanted to take together. After tender and loving vows were exchanged, the proclaiming of the two in holy matrimony, the happy couple dashed outside to the back seat of an awaiting limousine. The bride poked the groom with a finger.

"Were you nervous?"

Denton smiled. "Was I nervous? Naw, I was cool." Levitica gazed at him with suspicion. "Don't worry; I was nervous too." She replied and kissed her new husband. He reciprocated. For both, it was a dream come true.

While Denton continues his dreamlike journey down memory lane, a smile forms on his face recalling the beautiful fragments of a life he and Levitica shared. Recollections now shift to more troubling and challenging times. For as long as there is room for dreams, there must always be room for nightmares.

Like most families, Denton and his brother Edwin were involved in a sibling rivalry. The oldest Denton seethed over the attention and leniency his brother received. Perhaps a valid reason in Denton's point of view is that his father favored Edwin rather than himself. In high school, Edwin was an all-city fullback in football, leader of the honor society, etc. Adding insult to injury, Edwin attracted all the ladies with his cool demeanor and overwhelming confidence. In short, Edwin was 'it,' the one thing Denton could never measure up to. In contrast, Denton was quiet, reserved than his younger brother. He did have an intellectual edge as he pushed himself to

116

become an above-average student while Edwin struggled in the classroom. Nearly all of his life, Denton fought Edwin's solid popularity and influence, never receiving the level of respect he felt he deserved.

Because of his father's knowledge of his impending wedding to Levitica, Denton was "convinced" to not only invite Edwin but make him a member of the wedding party. Though it annoyed him, Denton went ahead with his father's wishes. In the wedding reception, after he exchanged vows with Levitica, Denton stood alone in the corner of the rented community center still in his tuxedo, hands in pockets, pondered a lingering question on his mind which he could not get rid of. Even though this day marked one of the happiest of his life, he lowers his head, asking over and over again, "Why can't I get along with Edwin?"

Three years after the wedding, Denton received news Edwin impregnated a young woman named Tisha, a sophomore in the same university in Northern California they attended. He heard the stories about her by his parents as a method of damage control. She was one of those 'fast girls,' constantly flirting with other men; his parents would state repeatedly as to sully her reputation and character to save Edwin's. Denton didn't believe their spin as he had taken a trip to the university without speaking with Edwin by not informing him of his presence, learned in a private conversation with her that she had a 3.8 G.P.A, planned to graduate with a business degree, and hopefully start a family with Edwin if their relationship lasted that far. She cried throughout the conversation, feeling betrayed and sorrowful she had an abortion because Edwin didn't want her child, which meant she could no longer have him. Denton assured her he believed her and would have his support. Levitica wasn't aware until the end of her life that

Denton secretly donated to Tisha's second try at a college degree monetarily, the one thing Edwin should have done.

Recalling all of this in the middle of his sleep disturbs Denton feeling the pangs of bitterness. Perhaps he would not have felt so vindictive towards his brother and would have forgiven the preferential treatment of him by their parents, the resentment of the manner he treated Tisha, only to almost destroy her life and that of the unborn child, but there was one more incident that he could never forgive his brother for. Unfortunately, this is a much significant reason why his relationship with Edwin is fractured if not almost non-existent.

The night Edwin was alone with Levitica.

One cold winter night in Denton and Levitica's apartment, Edwin steadily drank himself into a stupor. Denton believed Edwin wanted to drink because of an incident involving a young woman he knew and wanted to have a closer connection with; she told him to his face she didn't like nor needed to be with a man. Edwin immediately knew the reason why as he noticed hints about his friend that he consciously denied. Rather than guess all through the night whether or not his brother committed suicide, Denton against his better judgment, invited Edwin to keep an eye on him. He offered to drive Edwin home. He asked Levitica wearing a buttoned shirt and skirt, sitting on a couch to watch Edwin on the other side of their small living room slumped in a chair with a wine bottle in his hand. They both decided Edwin was too far gone to drive home. He lived only a few blocks away, near Buckingham Road and Santa Rosalia Drive. It wouldn't have been much for Denton to drive him back to his own apartment since he had his spare key. This wasn't the first time Denton had to drive him back under these conditions.

Levitica sat alone with Edwin while her husband warmed up the car outside. Just as Denton closed the door, she could feel the chilly air the rain produced on her face. It promptly revived Edwin, who sat upright, placing the bottle on the floor. Turning his head to stare at Levitica, who had been used to his impolite leering by his bloodshot eyes, Edwin began to stand up, nearly tripping over the coffee table. Levitica stood up to catch her brother-in-law from falling. He flashed a strange grin as she held him aloft, once again faced with a lustful look in his eyes.

"You know what, Levitica?" He slurred his words, continuing to look at her. Levitica felt queasy but knew she could not let him go.

"What is it?"

"You look tasty."

"You look drunk." Repulsed by his rude question, Levitica released her hold, allowing Edwin to stand up under his own power. He rubs his groin area playfully, bellowing out a sinister laugh that sickens her. "So? What does it matter to me? Come on, let's have a little play before Denton comes back. I want to have a peek under that sexy shirt." He pulled down his pants zipper. "I'll show you I'm more of a man than your husband. He doesn't deserve a fine thing like you...but I do."

"Are you sick? You're talking crazy, Edwin! Stay away from me!" Levitica shouted, avoiding Edwin's outstretched hands from unbuttoning her top. "How big are you, baby? I know you got some huge titties up there!" Edwin climbed on top of Levitica, pinning her captured body on the couch. She tried in vain to break free from his tight grip.

"Let me go!" She shouted while struggling to break free.

"You love me, don't you? You've always had, but you afraid to say it."

119

"Let me go! Denton!"

Again he asked, "You love me, right? Say it!"

"Please...please...let me go! Denton!"

"Say it bitch! Say you love me!" Edwin's strong hands tore away at the shirt ripping off pieces of her clothing.

"Stay away from her!" Denton returned, bolting through the door.

Edwin turned around, face displaying rage. "Damn you, nigga! What you are gonna do?"

A wild scuffle took place. Since Denton was the one in control of his senses, he won the fight over his physically stronger younger brother by landing a couple of fists on Edwin's head. Throwing him out, Denton issued a warning.

"This is the last time you will ever be in this place. I'm sorry your lesbian girlfriend broke your heart and all, and I don't care if you are my brother. If you ever come back here, I will beat your ass!" Hearing the loud and deeply toned threats of his brother, Edwin was forced to stumble back home in the fierce rainstorm alone, covering his head under his jacket. In his dazed and confused state, his injured pride could not cover the shame he had committed upon himself. Communication between the two brothers was almost nonexistent after the rape attempt. After Levitica's death and their father's, it improved..somewhat. That night was the beginning of many inescapable nightmares Denton recalls in his deep slumber. More are sure to follow.

Levitica and Denton were on the beach in the state of Washington one bright September morning on vacation, admiring the cool sparkling waves of the Pacific Ocean. Levitica possessed a few artistic talents. One of them was drawing, which she loved so much. It made her feel good to express herself through that medium. The happy couple walked on top of the golden sands holding hands. While they admired the crashing roar of the sea waves, Levitica watched an unusual bird in stride along the bright sand several feet away from her. "What's that?"

"I think it's an albatross. I learned about them from a poem in my English class. This is the first time I've seen one up close, and....hey baby girl, what are you doing?" Denton pulled his baseball cap over his eyes to block the sunlight affecting his view.

"Hush, I'm sketching it." Levitica removed her notepad and pencils from her duffle bag and began to draw. For five minutes, the albatross remained in clear sight. Levitica fought against a near-heavy wind blowing her flower-designed skirt through her legs. Denton smiled while his wife worked. He was impressed how she drew the bird with a quiet intensity, the same intensity which she showed her love for him. The albatross took a curious glance in their direction before it flew away. Levitica completed her sketch. Denton glanced at her finished work and smiled. "Say, baby girl, this is great! Let me congratulate you." He was about to embrace her, but she held back by placing a hand in the air. "Before you start thanking me for my artwork, I want to say thanks to you."

A confused Denton replied, "Thanks? For what?"

Calmly she said, "I'm pregnant."

"Are you sure? How long has it been?"

"Four weeks."

Denton smiled. "Congratulations!"

The couple surrounded each other in a loving embrace. Life never felt so good. Feeling the warm softness of her cheek, Denton made an overdue confession to his lovely wife. "I love you with all my heart, all I have to give." She almost burst into tears, wiping a slight bit of moisture from her face. "Denton, I felt it the first day I met you. I knew. I knew. I have always loved you, and I still do. For now, and forever."

For now, and forever.

The following months passed and with it, the happiness between the expectant couple deserved faded, turning into a nightmare. Levitica experienced sudden weight loss, including bouts of sickness from their trip, steadily growing worse in those months. One such episode happened one evening after dinner. She complained of an upset stomach, forcing her to clutch it in her hands while in pain.

"Oh, it hurts!"

Denton rushed to her side, holding her up. He felt helpless, unsure what to say or do to alleviate the pain. "You're going to be all right. Just relax."

"I'm trying. Please help me!"

The pain felt more severe, convincing enough for Denton to rush her to the hospital between mid-city and the Westside for an overnight stay. It was then Denton met with their physician, a Caucasian in his mid-fifties. He was shorter than Denton with a leaner build. His head showed signs of losing his black hair, almost bald. The news he shared didn't forecast a happy ending. Nestling in a leather seat in front of the physician's desk, Denton nervously placed his arms on the wooden armrest awaiting the results of Levitica's health. The physician entered the room. The look on his pale face was a sign to expect the worst.

"Mr. Rudolph," The physician named Dr. Chandler began by resting his elbows on the wooden tabletop, hands folded, his eyes straight ahead. "how long has your wife experienced her sickness?"

Denton gently searches his memories, head swaying back and forth. "Two weeks to a month now. Last night was the first time it has been that intense."

"Has she ever been checked for cancer? Looking up her family history, I recognized Levitica's mother had colon cancer. Levitica has a tumor in her ovary."

122

"So what are you saying?" Denton leans forward; his heart raced with shock and disbelief, hearing what caused his wife's sudden illness. The worst is yet to come.

"Your wife has ovarian cancer, Mr. Rudolph. Our tests confirm it. That would explain her weight loss."

"But she's pregnant with our first child. I thought she would gain weight instead of losing it. I've taken her to have a TVUS test not too long ago, and the doctors told me although they found tumors in her ovary, they agreed they were benign, not cancerous."

"Hmmm." Chandler leans back on his chair, searching in his mind to find an answer. "Depending on when you had the test done, Mr. Rudolph, chances are when it was taken, the doctors may find tumors as they did with your wife, but there's no way actually to predict they are cancerous or not." The physician leans again. He kept his hands folded, doing his best to remain calm, sharing his knowledge with a visibly upset Denton, who did his best to restrain his anger.

"Mr. Rudolph, our tests conclude Mrs. Rudolph has stage four, which is an advanced stage of her cancer. It has spread to her abdominal region and her liver. While we can hope for the best and do all we can on our end, there is the reality she won't make it. I'm sorry about this, Denton. I know how much you love her, and we'll do our best. Just be prepared if it turns out differently."

Denton's heart sank with an icy thud. He didn't want to accept what he had heard. He felt incapable of living now. It was as if a void opened up inside his soul. In four short years, his wife brought happiness into his life, and now hers was being lost. He had only one more question for the doctor. Fruitless, but hope drove the motivation to say it. His entire body trembled with a quiet fright. "What about the fetus...I mean the baby, will it live?"

There stood a moment of silence. Chandler removed his spectacles from his face, placing them in the palm of his hand. "Mr. Rudolph...I'm sorry to tell you this; it won't survive if it hasn't already. I'm sorry, truly sorry." The doctor left the room to clear out his dry throat and contain his sorrow.

Denton remained in the office alone, silently in his chair. He did not cry, didn't move, and didn't conjure vain thoughts of hope. He just sat there by himself with eyes directed outside, gazing at the sky.

Nothing mattered more to Denton but to enjoy his last days, hours, and seconds with his dying wife. He loved her with an unexplainable emotion that she cherished significantly. He spent each moment with Levitica like it was her last even though she suffered rapid weight loss, which meant the undeniable loss of their child. She knew unquestionably she would die soon, but Levitica also possessed a determined will. Sensing her life nearing an end, she focused on leaving a gift to her husband.

One night, Denton stood by the kitchen sink washing dishes. Levitica had a severe cramp, a symptom of her deteriorating condition. She slumped slowly to the floor below. Denton dashed to his wife's side, dropping a dish in the sink. Attempting to lift her now frail body, he felt Levitica push him away with her open hands. Again, he tried to help her up, but she refused. "I can take care of myself! I'm a grown woman! I may be dying, but I'm not helpless!" Levitica lifted herself, limped toward her husband already upset with himself, biting his lip. He felt unsure of how to comfort her. A tender hand slid under his defeated chin, rising her husband's bowed head.

"I'm sorry. I didn't mean to snap at you. I know this is just as difficult for you as it is for me." She told him, "Wait here." Levitica went into the closet and pulled out a painting of the albatross they saw at the beach. Denton

124

received Levitica's gift in his hands as she smiles at him. On the bottom, written on a tan background, an inscription read, *My soul is with yours forever.* Tears swelled in Denton's eyes. Levitica's watered too. It was one of the few times since that day they both had a chance to smile. Levitica bowed her head with satisfaction her mission was complete. Denton took his wife in his arms, grateful for having such a wonderful woman in his life. On that night, it was a perfect evening. Denton never wanted to end.

Finally, the night did come when Levitica's time in this world reached its final chapter. Once a treasured and prized woman, the now frail frame of Levitica laid on her deathbed awaiting her eternal rest. By her side, roses laid on the hospital bed. Denton firmly held her soft hands, never letting go. He knew his one true love would leave him, but he did not want to leave her. He bowed his head as he kissed his wife on the lips and forehead, offering a prayer of supplication in between. He did whatever he could do for her, but he realized he was helpless; that reality overwhelmed him as he hid his sorrow under a facade of bright smiles.

"Levitica, you look lovely." Her lips curved upward in response as she laid on her bed in a white smock, an unattractive image from the conservative clothing she wore to hide her once noticeable curvaceous body reduced to a gaunt figure on a hospital gurney. She recognized the irony as a cruel divine joke. She did believe she will see her parents again as she missed them greatly. They will be together again, although she felt hopeful the words she left for him in the painting would encourage Denton he will never be, nor feel alone.

"Thank you, Denton, but I want you to know I truly do love you."

With head bowed, Denton said, "I know."

125

"No. I want to tell you, so there won't be any doubt. The day I first saw you, I was in love. You brought so much joy into my life when there wasn't any. When all men wanted to do was enter my body but not my mind. I thank you for caring for me and always being by my side when I needed you. Denton, you were there for me period. The years I've spent with you on this earth, I could never be happier. I truly believe deep in my heart, no one in this world or the next will ever replace you Denton Rudolph, my sweet husband. I can rest knowing I had the honor of being your wife."

"Thank you." Denton did as best he could to hold back the oncoming tears.

"Don't cry. Whenever you ever feel sad and down, look at the painting, even the inscription. I will be with you forever. I pray my painting proves how much I want it to be true." Denton leaned over to give her a loving kiss. He stroked his wife's flowing hair. He continued to fight the tears in vain.

"We had perfect love, didn't we? You and I?"

"Yes, Denton, we did." Levitica grew weaker by the minute. "We did. Just remember, I will always love...."

Silence.

Her eyelids close for the final time. The light of life which he held in her hand faded rapidly. Although her passing took a few seconds, there was no denying Levitica had died.

No longer could Denton hold back his tears. A sudden tidal wave of grief swept over him as he kissed his departed wife on the forehead. Whispering, he uttered, "I'll always love you too, Levitica." He could not hold back his emotions any longer. That night, he held her in his arms one last time.

The loud ringtone of a smartphone returns Denton to the realistic and present world.

His eyes are flooded with tears, the result of the painful memories he revisited while he slept. He wipes them from his eyes, answering the phone on the bed next to him.

"Hello?"

"Hey Denton, it's Edwin. Listen, that buyer I told you who was interested in Levitica's painting wants to meet you. His name is Isaiah Hendricks, and he says to meet you at.........." Denton reluctantly reaches over to retrieve a notepad lying on a nightstand. He listens to and writes the information over the phone. After the conversation with his brother, Denton exits his bed, standing in front of the painting for several minutes. Even now, he remains undecided about what he should do with it. "Here comes the moment of truth." He pauses for a final gaze while reading the inscription, reflecting her final words to him and how much they meant. One quick turn to his left, Denton observes a bright object on Levitica's nightstand. With two fingers, he picks it up, placing it in his pants pocket. Thinking about what he picked up helps clear his thoughts somewhat, reflecting on the decision he must make. Realizing he must go through with the meeting, Denton removes the painting off the hinges carefully, covering it with a white sheet. On his way to meet Hendricks, his brain imagines several different scenarios of his final resolution. Although it was a difficult choice for him, he continues to question whether or not it will be the right one.

Denton arrives in the rapidly changing Leimert Park Village. His eyes scan the newest addition to the area, a Metro rail car rested near a platform as it undergoes a test run. Soon it will accept awaiting passengers along the freshly laid tracks. It will travel Southbound on Crenshaw

Boulevard to its final destination, the L.A. International Airport. So much has changed from the cultural hub he knew to the latest stop for millennial hipsters of a different ethnicity than the people who used to assemble in the nearby park on Forty Third Place. Parking his car near the intersection of Forty Third Street and Degnan Boulevard, Denton steps out of his vehicle, promptly slipping a couple of quarters in the meter adjacent to his vehicle. He believes his visit will not take long. Opening the rear door, he slowly removes the painting from the back seat's floor with a sheet still draped over it. His eyes turn upward on Degnan, Denton begins the long walk towards the gallery across the street.

During his brief stroll towards the art gallery, Denton's eyes witness the sudden changes to Leimert around him. The Lucy Florence coffee house closed its doors a long time ago, only a memory to individuals who attended the establishment or heard of it. The location of the World Stage switched sides. Its previous location seems to be undergoing a bit of a transformation along with the other row of near-empty storefronts occupying its former space. The transition may be the order of the day at the village, but not all of the old cultural, artsy stores had vanished. He stops short of reaching Forty Third Place when he turns and steps inside a small, dimly lit store with an air of incense. Denton notices numerous paintings from local artists hanging on the walls, vases, and jewelry held in glass display cases. He nervously approaches the young college woman with a pecan brown complexion brushing off lint from her head twisted in locks behind a glass counter. Spotting Denton, she flashes a friendly smile.

"Hello." Her voice sounds pleasant, calming. Her eyes gleam with excitement. Denton feels nervous, lowering the painting as not to let the sweat from his hands

128

ruin it. His pores open up, releasing more sweat. He feels it drenched on his back.

"Hello there." In a faint voice, Denton asks, "Is Mr. Hendricks in? I have an appointment with him to take a look at this painting for sale." Denton's feet feel numb, almost frozen. His heart questions his decision (or was it Edwin's?) of selling Levitica's artwork. *What would it accomplish? What's the reason for this? Would I have sold the painting if she were alive?* An inner battle rages within Denton, harshly confronting his conscience, juggling between solutions back and forth. He hears the heavy footsteps of an older Black gentleman emerging from a string of long beads covering the rear entrance, facing his nervous customer. The older gentleman is tall and slightly thin, wearing a vest over a long-sleeved shirt. His head has noticeably grey hair on top, while the hair on his mustache and beard are black. The older gentleman leans toward Denton to shake his hand just as Denton eliminates queries arising in his mind and the nervousness he senses. He reaches to accept the firm, manly handshake of the older gentleman standing across from him. Denton feels the tight, secure handshake from his elder counterpart, full of confidence. The elder stares right into Denton's eyes with a quiet determination.

"Mr. Hendricks?"

"The one and only." Mr. Hendricks's voice reveals a subtle Jamaican accent mixed with American. "You must be the young man your brother told me about. I believe you have something to show me." Denton observes the young girl at the front desk staring back towards him with a smile as she answers phone calls from customers.

Before he uncovers the painting to show him, Denton faces Mr. Hendricks. The elder's eyes swiftly notice the disparity in height between the two. Denton briefly sees it, then proceeds with his question. "How do you know my brother? I'm just curious."

"I met him at a street festival on Degnan a few weeks ago. Funny, now that these white people are moving in, it looks like our festivals will be a thing of the past. I'm sorry, let me answer your question. Your brother and I spoke for quite a while after I told him I buy paintings. They have to be of high quality, you know. If I'm planning to stay here in the village, I need to have the best painting these folks can afford and, at the same time, give these local artists a chance to have their work shown. I'm sorry again, young man, what is your name, and would you like to have some water?" Hendricks walks a few steps to take out two bottles of water from his cooler a few feet away. Stretching with one long arm, he passes one to Denton.

"Denton, and yes, I would." Denton receives his bottle, opens the top, and takes a sip.

"Things are changing quite a bit. You see that new rail line down here, don't you? White folks will say that's progress; I say there ain't nothing left for us Black folks here. Oh, I know, we have our festivals and cultural events, but those Jewish folks still own the property, even this building where I operate my business. As long as they own this and see that new clientele come in....well, it doesn't make a difference, doesn't it? I just received my "eviction notice" last week from the property owner. It looks like this shop won't be here much longer. Just the way those folks like it." Denton recognizes the half resignation in Hendrick's eyes; a feeling of remorse for what he once had is now being lost. Quietly reflecting on his own decision, Denton faintly compares his situation with that of Mr. Hendricks without the sense of resignation. Whereas Mr. Hendricks could feel the sense of community leaving him replaced by something unknown, Denton attempts to relate

130

to losing Levitica only to find himself in a life without her, also mysterious.

"Let's get back to business. It looks like you have a painting to sell. Is that true?" Denton takes a side look at the sheet, nodding silently. He does all he could to convince himself that he is doing the right thing giving it to Hendricks. "At least there will be no more pain." He thought. He hands over the painting, albeit slowly. Hendricks glances at it with critical eyes. He sounds pleased, nodding his head several times. "This is a fantastic work of art! You paint very well."

"It's not mine."

"Whose is it then? This is talent!"

"It's from my wife. She passed away months ago."

Hendricks pauses, feeling numb. "Oh...I see." The art dealer is taken aback by the revelation. "Mr. Rudolph, are you sure you're still willing to sell it to me? I mean, this is a lovely piece and....." He could not find words to finish the rest of his sentence.

"Yes, I am." Denton lowers his tone.

"How much do you want for it?" Hendricks asks for a price, but somewhere inside Denton, the conflict within his soul surfaces.

Hendricks waits for an answer.

The tortured Denton thinks in his mind, "Why am I doing this? She painted it for me." His mind repeats the words Levitica expressed to him via the inscription, "My soul is with yours forever."

Forever. A weird sense of calm sweeps over Denton for a minute, rendering him motionless. Slapping his pants, Denton feels an object inside his pocket. He pulls it out slowly and stares at Levitica's wedding ring, holding it up to his eyes for a minute. His face shows no expression as his mind is deep in thought. Amazed, Hendricks stands motionless, observing his guest stare at the bright ring gleaming as it hits the light. Finally, Denton nods his head and grins. He has the answer he needs.

"Mr. Rudolph, Denton, are you alright?" Hendricks asks with a bit of concern.

Denton takes a deep breath to stare at the painting briefly. He turns directly towards Hendricks, still holding the wedding ring in the air. "Mr. Hendricks, sir, I think I've looked this all wrong."

Hendricks shakes his head, taking a step back. "What makes you say that?"

"This morning when I woke up, I wasn't sure whether or not I would sell this painting, although I wouldn't have felt bad if I let it go. Then I stared at Levitica's nightstand and saw her wedding ring. I asked myself, why doesn't the ring make me feel just as sad? She wore it; it was on her finger; it reminds me of her every time I see it. Then I realized maybe it's not the painting or the ring after all. Maybe I thought so much of her death, but not about the painting, her ring, which reminds me of the love we shared. Levitica poured her dying heart and soul into that painting as a reminder she'll always be with me. Her death became my burden, my albatross, you might say. Now I see I shouldn't grieve because she's physically gone. She'll always be with me in my heart and mind. I can remember the day she put on her wedding ring. She had the biggest smile…." Denton bends over and cries. "I loved her so much……. oh baby, I will always love you!"

Moved, Hendricks takes a step closer to Denton, comforting him. "It's all right, young man. What you said is true. That woman of yours may not be there to hold you anymore, but it's the memories, the good times you were together, that you have to hold on to. I've been reading that description in the painting, and for sure, she shows her love for you through that art. She loved you a lot, son. A whole lot."

"That's why I can't sell it. It may be crazy to say that, and I don't mean to waste your time, but this is a gift from my wife. I can't give it up."

Hendricks nods. "I know. You haven't wasted my time, but I'm proud of you for recognizing the gift your wife left you. I hope you cherish it as much as you cherished her."

I think that every work of art here has a value which is why I sell them. You showed me that life has more value than what we think." Hendricks backs away and offering one last piece of wisdom to Denton. "You are a fortunate young man to realize your wife didn't have to create this work of art for you. She could have felt sorry for herself; you as a man would have shared in that grief, and the both of you would have had a miserable end. But the more I look at this, the more I see the love. I see her soul into this. Look at the features of this bird...."

"She did an outstanding job," Denton adds.

"Every detail is intricate, flawless. She went out of her way to show you how much she loved you. You were a very fortunate young man to have deserved a woman such as her. I'm sorry for your loss, but I believe by the way you've been speaking to me, it looks like you've found her again. Please promise me you will never think of selling this painting, ever."

"I won't, sir, and.... thank you."

"Good luck Denton. I hope your life's journey is a good one no matter what happens." Hendricks extends his hand. Denton is reluctant at first but reaches out to shake it firmly. Hendricks's eyes show a touch of remorse for Denton's loss but are relieved he found the answer he sought, which gives him peace.

Denton covers the painting with the sheet again and promptly leaves Hendricks, who resumes his regular duties inside the store. Feeling relieved for the first time in months, Denton slips his painting inside his car, driving back to his apartment with a smile on his face. The suffering has disappeared.... for now. Denton understands it will not be easy to remove the pain of Levitica's death completely, but he is determined not to be a slave to it any longer.

The following day, Edwin picks up the phone in his apartment. "Hello?" he asks to lean back in a chair, feet kicked back.

"Edwin, this is Denton. Can you come over here? We need to talk."

An hour and a half later, Denton answers his doorbell. Standing at the front door, Edwin unzips his jacket, waiting for his brother to let him in. Once inside, he glances at the living room wall. The painting hangs in its usual place. Next to it was a photograph of Denton and Levitica arm in arm with each other.

"You kept it, huh?"

"Yes."

Edwin walks over to his brother, who stands near the painting. Edwin lowers his head with a gentle nod, signaling he respects Denton's decision. "Denton, I just..........."

"After I left Mr. Hendricks's store, I took time to wonder why you wanted me to sell the painting beside you getting something out of it. You knew how much I was hurting inside, and you wanted to help me. I suppose if you hated me at all, you wouldn't have done anything about it, but you wanted to help take that pain away from me. Edwin, I thought long and hard about what happened between you and Levitica. You were going through your pain and because I......"

Edwin holds up the palm of his hand. "Let me stop you right there, big brother. I can't let you easily forgive me for

134

what I've done. I messed up, pure and simple. Levitica was your wife. I just wanted to get out of control that night. I wanted to die, for real. Approaching her like that, saying what I said to her…. that was out of line. I disrespected her, and I disrespected you. I can't be excused for what I've done. All I want to do is be a better man, a strong Black man, and own up to my mistakes. I just want to put things right with the people I've hurt."

"Like Tisha?"

"Yeah, definitely her. I know you've helped her out paying her way through college. Levitica told me before she died. I didn't know why she would do that since I disrespected her, but I imagine she wanted me to know. You did what a man is supposed to do and you proved it. You stepped up to the plate Denton; I didn't. Now it's about time for me to make sure I do right by others and just be a man. I just don't to be only a man, Denton, but I want to be your brother again."

"I would like that," Denton says cracking a smile. "If you need Tisha's phone number and email address, I can give that to you. I don't know if she'll want to talk or see you again. It's been so long."

"I know." Edwin lowers his head. "If anything, all I want to do is to tell her how sorry I am for messing up her life. She can live with whatever man she's with, but I need to let her know that. I want to apologize and move on."

"If you want to be a man like you say you are, then I'll help you, no problem."

Edwin nods with a grin. "Thank you so much. I needed to hear that from you. From now on, I promise to make it right. I hope you know that."

"I do." Denton crosses his arms, grinning. "I know it's going to be all right." Step one in the healing process was completed. How far they will go, no one knows. At least the effort will be genuine this time.

Later in the evening, Denton decides to grab a bite to eat at the Revolution Café. Searching for his jacket, a sudden realization hits him. For the time being, he will be alone. Nevertheless, as he told Mr. Hendricks, he is free. Free to move on with his life. That assurance convinces Denton to continue living, knowing the problematic social adjustments he must face.

Outside his apartment, Denton gazes at the starlit sky above. Focusing on it, Denton imagines a picture of an albatross such as the one in his apartment. Next to the image is the face of his dearly departed wife. Her features were as bright as the heavens above. He wasn't quite sure, but he believes she blows a kiss at him. Looking down on her husband, her lips part with "I love you."

He blows a kiss back to her and grins. Joy has returned to his life. Then one last time, he speaks to Levitica's image. "Goodbye, baby, I will love you with all my heart, always." With those words, Denton turns towards the street and walks away.

Lift Up Your Veil

Lift up your veil, Sista
I know you had
your drama with men
who refuse to treat you well
not appreciating you for the woman
you were made to be
I ask that you raise up
protective mask
peace and freedom
can be yours if only
you're up to the task.

I plead to you raise your veil
for I'm one of the brothers
not thrown behind jail cell
I saved up my money with everything I had
I spent it all for my tuition in college
so that I may elevate
as an educated man
to acquire knowledge
studying to earn that degree
of course, I did it
for myself no doubt but also to prove
I have more to offer if only you see.

All I seek is to lift your cloak of unhappiness
to show you the many ways
you've been blessed

I would love you so
taking you on a trip to Paradise
the way I would cater to you
makes you think
about your opinion of men, twice.

I'd shower you with affection
a hug, kiss
a gentle whisper in your ear
sharing you my heart
of things I hold dear
I would be committed to you
enjoying the ways
love can and should be
never letting go
to the rest of our living days.

So sista
it is your decision
I poured out my soul
in honest petition
I pray after revealing that I am a man
who will respect, treat you well
you'd find it in your heart
by greeting me with a smile
lifting that veil.

Remembering The Nights

I remember the nights
locked in a tight embrace
feeling the heat
of your womanly form
the way you held me
next to you
made me secure and warm
I recall the perfume
you used to wear
appropriately named
Sweet Fragrance
listening to slow jams
all through the night
swaying in a slow dance.

I still see your eyes
calm and soothing
like diving in
a deep loving pool
I smile at the times
we both made jokes
which was the best part
of being with you, all mine
I hear the words
we both vowed
no matter what season
of weather
we'd do our best

to make each other happy
supporting our hopes
and dreams
together.

Yes baby
I still think back
on the good times
overcoming the bad
those days will
come around soon
no reason for us
to be sad
just writing this letter
to you on a warm night
in September
saying I love you
with all, I have to give
it's those special moments
we shared
that I will most remember.

Come home soon. I miss you.

Help Meet

Help Meet
walk by my side
not with control
or subversion
but with equal pride
lend an ear
for my pain
share my voice
in a time of trouble
let peace be your choice
give an embrace
merge with my soul
so that we may
become one
unified in everything
till our days are done.

Reaching Out

It's the middle of the night
the sky is lit up
stars shining bright
there is one thing
even harsher than the cold
the fact you're not in my life baby
for my arms to hold.

I stretch out my hand
upwards toward the stars
hoping I touch your heart
no matter how far
praying you to feel
my extended fingertips
that's all I can do
since I can't taste your lips
anymore.

I pull back my hand
ball it up in a fist
hold it over my chest
pretending it was your tender head
where it used to rest
my eyes stay closed
I refuse to look at the reality
of you no longer
sharing this night with me.

You're gone forever
from my life baby
if things had been better between us
then just maybe -
no, I can't pretend
I have to accept
what my heart knows is true
you have a man now
made only for you.

So on this cold evening
again I look at the stars
reaching out once more
I wanted you to know I loved you
with all my might
but as I leave, I pray
just as the stars are aligned
your new union
will turn outright
you've found a man
all of this stormy weather
farewell baby
I sincerely hope you two
are happy forever.

Do Fries go with That Snake?

Brushing her long windblown hair with a fresh pedicured hand, model Lynn Dumont smiles completing yet another photoshoot. It was held in Exposition Park near the National History Museum for a new startup magazine she is excited to participate in. In her hand returning to her Jeep Wrangler is a cage concealing a six-foot boa constrictor named Baby. The photoshoot manager learned from past conversations with Lynn she loves snakes and has Baby as a pet due to her boyfriend, a former professional athlete and up-and-coming entrepreneur. The photographer invited her to take her pet along for additional pictures for the shoot in a small park in front of the museum. Lynn wears bright-colored biking shorts and a tank top while the rest of her exposed glowing butter pecan skin glows, smiling the entire time, holding Baby in her hands delicately.

After the session, Lynn places the cage in the jeep's rear, making sure Baby is secure and safe. Jumping in her driver's seat, she sways her head back and forth mindlessly to the music jams of a new 'old school' rhythm and blues station in the city. Exiting the parking lot adjacent to Bill Robertson Lane on her way towards Exposition Boulevard close by, Lynn's stomach growls due to hunger. She deprived herself of food before the shoot, and now she feels the urge to put something in her tummy. "Baby, you hungry?" Lynn speaks to her pet playfully.

Baby hisses, not able to express its tastes for mice Lynn feeds it constantly. "Mama's very hungry; she knows that. Let's see; we can go to Subway. No go, huh? How about Chipotle? Not there either? Where then? The Burger Palace? Are you sure? It's fast food, and Mama doesn't agree with that greasy stuff, but I guess I can cheat a little bit. Okay, we'll go there."

Before Lynn's arrival, Brandon Clark lays his large duffle bag near the door of his South Los Angeles home in the Chesterfield Square district. He wears a noticeable work attire of an orange and blue Burger Palace uniform with a name tag above his chest. He fiddles with hooking a miniature gold chain around his neck. His grandfather rests in an easy chair in the spacious living room watching a television show on one of the digital subchannels providing his favorite series.

"I guess you're going to work to talk to that Polly girl." His grandfather spoke, using his remote control near his armrest to turn the television off.

"Yeah Pappy, you're right. Today I'm finally going to ask her to go on a date with me if things work out. She just broke up with our manager, and now she's single."
Brandon slid in the claps to his chain, hooking it around his neck.

"She broke up with your manager? Boy, you sure you want to look for another job?" His grandfather sits up, giving Brandon a puzzled look in his eyes.

"Relax Pappy," Brandon holds a hand in the air. "We all knew it was coming anyway. You see, they weren't all that serious…."

"Never mind that." His grandfather shakes his head. "If you plan to go out with this Polly girl, be sure your cousin who is the manager I have to add, is okay with you making a move on her so soon. Otherwise, he might fire you, and then the next thing you know, you'll get that technical job you want in Playa Vista with Facecrook."

145

"That's Facebook Pappy, not Facecrook, and that's not who I would be working for." Brandon corrects him.

"Sorry about that boy. You know I can't keep up with all these unsocial media you young people are into today. Trust me; I've seen your mama on that thing, fussing with folks and all. Just like on that Twatter, she was passing along a story about that good-looking girl who can't sing, but...."

"You mean Twitter, and I know you're not talking about her. You know mama's a big fan of that singer you're dissing, so we better chill."

"What is it with you young people and this unsocial media? You know a young man at the nursing home was showing pictures...."

"Selfies, Pappy. They're called selfies."

"... on his Instant Sham and all I saw were these four beautiful Black girls flaunting their big breasts and butts on there just smiling and all. Why do y'all get to snap pictures at everything? Most of y'all don't need to have your pictures snapped, period! Too many ugly people in this world, and nearly all of them on that Instant Sham showing their hoos hoos and stuff!"

"Pappy...." Brandon knew his grandfather spoke of a website similar to the one he mentioned, but he shakes his head. He hid his chuckle with a smile, "I'll see you later."

"Take it easy, Brandon. Maybe I'll see you on that thing they call My Place if you take a picture at work."

Carrying his duffle bag with regular clothes inside, Brandon unlocks his front door and heads out. He heaves the bag over his shoulders with such ease it would confuse anyone why a slender young man such as himself would handle a heavy object. Despite his body frame, Brandon possesses enough strength to endure the short walk from his house to the bus stop. He waves to his neighbor Mrs.

Phillips. Brandon approaches the slender older Black woman watering her front lawn before passing her by on the way to his bus stop down the street.

"Don't waste too much water, Mrs. Phillips, before the DWP (Department of Water and Power) blames you for our next great drought."

"I won't, dear." Mrs. Phillips laughs. "How's your grandfather?" Water splashes on her bright shirt.

Brandon laughs in return. "He's okay, but I think he has trouble with this new thing called technology. It may be too fast for him."

Mrs. Phillips cracks a smile. "I guess he's not as hip as us young people."

"I guess not; see you later, Mrs. Phillips."

On his way to the Burger Palace on Figueroa Street between Exposition Boulevard and Martin Luther King, Jr. Boulevard, Brandon waits at his stop twenty minutes for a local bus to arrive. While he waits, he thinks how he is close to finishing his general courses at L.A. Southwest College and would earn enough money to buy his car to apply for a new startup multimedia company in the heart of Playa Vista known as 'Silicon Beach.' He wishes hopefully they will approve and offer him a job. However, that was in the future. For the present, he works at the Burger Palace to get through college despite rumors of its impending closure. Brandon knew in the long run, he would have the last laugh. He would have a good-paying job, and his doubters would be the ones left out on the streets.

One bus ride and half an hour later, Brandon enters the Burger Palace with only a few customers in their seats. His manager and cousin Clyde checks his watch. "Well, well, isn't this something? The homie's on time today." Brandon stares at the well-dressed Clyde in his buttoned shirt and tie. "Yeah, someone has to do all the work here." The manager sneers at his cousin. "That was weak, weakling.

147

Get to work." Brandon didn't like Clyde too much growing up, and the dislike continues into their adulthood. It's more of a playful dislike, not too serious.

According to the great Clyde himself, he was all-world at Crenshaw High School, even more popular than the great basketball players winning state titles. He played football at the Shaw, then because no Division I school dared not to fully utilize his talent (or the headache that came with it), he played for L.A. Southwest College and then UC San Diego. The way Clyde describes it, he was the victim of an ongoing conspiracy denying him playing time. As he vividly recalls his fondest moments as a player on the sidelines griping to anyone who'd listen:

See, if the coach put me in, we'd win this game!
Look at that sorry tailback! And he's starting over me?
Come on, coach! It's Washington Prep; you gotta start me! They ain't won since white folks danced to disco music!
Naw, naw, don't worry! Coach is just saving me for the big plays. Let ole number twenty-four get most of them carries; I'm good, I'm straight!
Dang man! I hate this school! How am I going to show the NFL I'm a number one draft pick?

His call to greatness ended when the local team of a disbanded spring football league cut him – before their first game! Clyde feels even to this day; there were haters who plotted his exit from the team, not appreciating his awesome skills as a running back/linebacker. They didn't know what they were missing! Clyde's boasted many times. The team who cut him won the first (and only) championship in the new league, so they may not have missed him that much. Now through one of his ex-

148

teammates, he's the manager of the Burger Palace. Maybe it's not what he expected, but he has a job, and that's all he cares about.

Truthfully, no one at the fast-food place cared for Clyde to begin with. He's described as pushy, demanding, stuck up, and a bit of a sexist. The ladies hate him with a passion, no matter how much Clyde wanted to show his 'softer side' around them. He used to date one unfortunate young woman, Polly Rogers. "Sweet Polly," as she was called, works in the drive-through booth, whereas Brandon takes orders at the counter. Brandon couldn't form a clear picture in his mind of Polly's physical features because her uniform hid her shape, but he imagines it matches her beautiful face, stunning without make-up. Oftentimes, she flashes a smile that melts Brandon's heart. As she passes by the beverage dispenser, Brandon said hello to her.

"Hey Brandon, what's going on?" Polly flashes her precious smile at him.

"I heard from the grapevine that you and someone we know have gone your separate ways. Is that true?"

"Well, it's true. I used to think we could work things out between us if someone were a bit more...sensitive to the people around him. Then I found out that person has issues I can't even read, so I decided to let him go."

"Say if someone really liked you and could be sensitive to you, would you give him an opportunity to know you better?" Brandon asks.

"Hmm.... that depends. You see Brandon, as much as I can't figure out, I still have feelings for Clyde, shocking as it is. It's not as easy to build up a relationship with one person after they break up with someone else. It takes time, you know?"

"Yeah, I know." Brandon feels the confident air sucked out of him.

"Better get back to the window before you-know-who finds out I'm not there. See you later."

"Take care, Polly."

Local community leader and businessman Abdul Saeed stares across the street the former L.A. Memorial Sports Arena site, torn down and rebuilt to become a new soccer stadium for the city's newest professional team. Taking a couple of puffs on his cigarette with ashes falling on a Black hand, the owner over fifty years of age with an olive complexion and a streak of gray noticeable in his hair leans against his BMW continuing to puff on his cigarette. He curiously watches the construction crew across Figueroa hard at work, spending long hours to complete this project his business will not profit from moving forward. In his years taking over ownership of the Burger Palace after the L.A. Olympics of years past, Saeed takes pride in his own as his father, who bought the rights from the original owner, handed control over to him. He only has control of this location out of several Burger Palaces throughout the city. Firmly committed to the community, Saeed remained steadfast in his vow to stay throughout events that could have forced him to close down earlier or move, such as gang violence and the L.A. Unrest.

He shrugs his slender shoulders under his sports jacket waiting outside the parking lot in his BMW, awaiting Clyde to step out so he could give him the bad news. The bright sunlight shines brightly on his skin. His eyes squint when he observes Clyde walking out to greet him. He lowers his hand with the cigarette. With a free hand, he extends it to shake Clyde's. He forces a smile to put up a false front; all is well before Clyde hears the bad news he has just received.

"What's up, Mr. Saeed? What did you find out?" Clyde exchanges a fist bump with him.

"We close down in two weeks. The family trust decided to let this location go because we felt the property values will skyrocket once the soccer stadium is finished leaving us no choice but to shut down operations. We could stay and try to fight it out, but the city's changing Clyde, and after forty years at this same location, why waste time and money?" Clyde nods, totally understanding Mr. Saeed.

"We have other projects to focus on, including an acquisition of a struggling community newspaper, so we'll be fine. Can I trust you to call a meeting today and let everyone know? We'll see what we can do to give them their two weeks pay."

"You got it, Mr. Saeed. Are you going inside?"

"No, I only stopped by to talk to you. I have a meeting with the family in thirty minutes. I should be back before closing time to see how everyone's feeling."

"Don't worry, Mr. Saeed." Clyde raises a hand. "I'll let everyone know today. I'll make sure of that."

Brandon daydreams of Polly without realizing the strawberry shake he's filling in a large paper cup begins to overflow to his hand... The shake oozes all over it, landing on the floor in a big mess. "Dog!" He whispers in obscenities in frustration. Clyde returns from his visit with Mr. Saeed, noticing the error.

"You're slipping, cousin." Tormenting Brandon as he loves to do, Clyde taps him on the shoulder with a smirk on his face. Brandon turns around with a new shake already made, passing it to his customer waiting at the long counter. He approaches Clyde on the side, shaking his head. "Better keep your mind on your job."

"I'll do that, cousin. I saw you talking with Mr. Saeed outside. What did he tell you?"

"In due time." Clyde takes a step back from Brandon as to not to give him clues of his conversation. "I'll have a meeting with y'all before closing tonight to go over what we discussed."

"I'll make it a point to be right here."

"Make sure you're on point, period. No slip-ups like the shake you just spilled."

Waving at Polly as she passes by, Brandon felt the possibility of ever dating her was slim because of his short stature of five foot six, two inches taller than Polly. *Maybe I'm not the one to please her if Polly likes tall guys. Dag, she liked Clyde, so it can't be that bad, still...*

A co-worker, Francine, shares register duty with Brandon. Not only is she Polly's close friend, but a recent winner in a local radio station's contest for free tickets to an upcoming Old School music festival featuring the famous singer Johnny Gill. When the flow of customers died down and an air of brief silence fills the fast-food restaurant, Brandon asks her, "Francine, what type of man does Polly like? What do you think?"

Francine shrugs her shoulders, unsure. "I don't know, why?" Her cocoa butter hand slides across the counter with a towel, wiping off moisture.

"What I'm trying to say is, do you think she likes me?"

"I suppose. Brandon, you'll have to ask her yourself. I know when I go backstage to that Old School Festival, I will finally see Johnny Gill, a man whom I have lusted over faithfully for years. I'm going to walk right up in front of Johnny and say, "you are my man, you belong to me!" And baby," Francine snaps her fingers high in the air as she proclaims, "I dare the first thing coming after Johnny when I get with him will be turned away whether it'll be man, woman or beast."

Brandon interjects, "Speaking of beasts........."

Clyde approaches Francine on her left side. "Well, sexy Francine, I heard you're going to the Old School Festival. Need some company?"

152

The fairly attractive and healthy young woman in her mid-twenties changes her facial expression with a hostile stare. "I would rather invite a dirty dog with one eye infested with fleas and ticks."

"What time do you want me to pick you up?"

Francine sighs and shakes her head, shooting down Clyde's offer with an extended palm in the air. As soon as he left, Brandon said to Francine, "Looks like you rubbed him the wrong way."

"Whatever!" Francine laughs, pausing to stare right at Polly. "Girl, what was wrong with you dating him?"

Polly places a hand on her chin. "Hmm, I believed the hype, I guess."

In the present, Lynn's jeep arrives at the fast-food restaurant. Her jeep's engine hums as she muses over her choices in the drive-through line. "Well Baby, that didn't take long did it? We had to wait a while because of that construction, but we made it." Trying to decide whether she should stay, seeing the long line of vehicles ahead of her, Lynn makes her choice. "Darn it! Guess I have to park. Line's too long." She parks her jeep near the open back door. Briefly turning her head, she speaks to what she assumes is Baby resting in its cage in the rear. "Now Baby, mama's just going to take a second. I'll be right back." Lynn locks the driver's side door. In her haste to grab a bite to eat, she forgot to lock Baby's cage, allowing it to slither away from the jeep as Lynn rushes inside the Burger Palace. She stands silent, watching another long line of customers waiting for their order. She makes a decision out of frustration to return to her jeep and drive to another fast-food restaurant nearby. While Lynn goes back to her jeep, the unseen Baby slithers its way to the Palace's unlocked back door. It quietly makes its way inside the men's restroom sneaking past the door slightly ajar, resting behind the toilet seat. Shadows hid its form.

153

The moment of truth has arrived for James, part of the crew to clean the restrooms. His pail bangs against a closed door, causing a loud sound. He feels the water inside the bucket splashing on his charcoal-like complexion. Pulling out his mop, he prepares to wet the floor. As he is about to perform his chore, he hears a faint hissing noise. "Man, y'all trying to play tricks on me again, huh?" James turns his head from side to side, believing his co-workers are pulling a prank on him. "I ain't even trippin' Ivan and Angela; you can't joke a jokester." James pokes his head out the door. The mop handle lands on the floor near Baby, and its head jumps forward, lunging towards James. His eyes widened.

"What the..."

Before he could get over his shock, Baby recoils its head, appearing to lunge again—James bolts out of the restroom. "Help! It's after me!"

'Queen Angela,' as she is known among the crew, is a young student attending junior college with eyes to match her caramel skin tone. Her duty is to empty the wastebaskets, a task interrupted by James running towards her on the side of the restaurant. His face is drenched with fear and sweat. He leans next to her. "Hey Angela, come with me." She doesn't understand what James is telling her through his heavy breathing, words hard to understand. "There's something I have to show you."

"You know I'm busy, James. Didn't Clyde tell you about cutting out the pranks? I don't have time to play around with you."

"Please Angela, this is serious. You won't believe this, but there's a snake in the men's restroom!"

"That's nice, James." She says dismissively. "I don't want to get in trouble again. If you and Ivan are playing a joke, I'm not interested."

James waves his hands frantically, begging Angela to go with him. "This ain't a joke. Just come with me, please?"

James and Angela walk to the men's restroom to find…. "Nothing! But where, how? It was here a minute ago and tried to attack me." A shocked and embarrassed James utters curse words staring behind the toilet, peeking around to see where Baby could have gone. His face displays a look of disbelief.

"You know what? I think you need serious help. If you excuse me, I have to get back to work so Clyde won't yell at me." Angela leaves in a huff back to her task.

James scratches his head, asking himself, "That's funny. I thought it was here. I wonder where that snake could be?"

Baby slinks its way slowly across the dimly lit hallway to the adjacent open door of the food storage area. Ivan is a slender young man with a goatee, known for playing the most practical jokes on his co-workers. He enters the small room walking over a tile floor. His eyes scan to see the silver shelves stacked with several plastic containers on top of the smooth surface. He hears a hissing noise near the freezer, approximately a few feet away from him. He raises his ears to hear the hissing for a second time. He concludes it's James paying him back for an earlier practical joke in which he was the victim. He stretches out his long thin arms outward, taking cautious steps towards the freezer so he wouldn't be taken by surprise. He adjusts his glasses on his nose by pushing them upward to get a better look.

"I wonder who that is." Baby hid in plain sight under the freezer, so Ivan assumes James is setting him up. The young Latino male looks forward, heart beating just a tad as the hissing grows louder the closer Ivan approaches the freezer.

"Ah-ha James, I got you - get away from me!"

Baby lunges up toward Ivan, missing his feet. He ducks, thinking Baby might strike his chest. Francine enters the area, searching for an extra tray for a customer. In fright, Ivan bumps into her, almost knocking her off her feet. Promptly, Francine faces him with a confused look on her face. "What's the matter with you? You act like you've seen a ghost."

With quivering lips, Ivan says, "How about a snake? It's here!"

Francine stands straight up, snaps her fingers high in the air, and said, "Ooooooo, help me! The next thing you'll say is that dirty low-down reptile is right behind me."

Hiss!

Francine hears the sound. Her eyes suddenly register shock. Glancing downward, she stares with icy fear as Baby coils around her ankles. "Yow!" She exclaims, leaping by Ivan as Baby slithers away. They dash to the front counter terrified, running past the long lines of tired and hungry customers. Clyde throws up his hands in frustration, incensed. He takes an angry stride to Francine and Ivan, huffing and puffing in an empty booth, shouting at them. "What the hell are you two doing?"

"We saw a snake in the back. You better take care of it." Francine speaks with a shaky voice.

"Ooooooo, help me!" Clyde mocks Francine's catchphrase with an air of sarcasm. "Is that why you two decided to run out to the dining area and play around? You're both five seconds from being fired."

Ivan warns Clyde, facing them with a physically imposing stance, "If you fire us, you can fire the snake too."

"What? Ivan, don't clown me. Where is this 'snake'?" Clyde's question is answered, for suddenly Baby slithers in clear view for everyone to see. The forty or so customers bolt toward the front and side exits in a mad rush. The brave souls who stay behind use their smartphones to post the disruption on their social media profiles and websites. Clyde, in vain, desperately urges each person with a smartphone out to put them away, but it was too late. The scene had already gone viral. Despite this, Clyde possesses an air of calm and demonstrates it by brushing lint off his shirt. He said to the people remaining inside, "Are you afraid of a little something like this? I'll grab this thing barehanded." Strutting with a confident shake in his walk, Clyde confronts Baby face to face.

Here is where each takes their stand—man to reptile. Clyde prepares to do battle with this snake chasing away his customers. He bends down, staring at his intruder with cold steel eyes, ready to do whatever it takes to remove it out of sight. With a deep voice, he orders, "All right you, you reptile. I'll give you five seconds to get out of here." Baby hissed to what one could interpret as a human laugh. Now feeling a little nervous and a bit restless, Clyde nervously starts his countdown.

"One."

Baby hissed.

"Two. Come on now, leave!"

Baby hissed louder.

"Three. Dang, move, move!"

Baby's head jerks back.

"Four. Aw, let's go, let's go!"

Baby lunges towards Clyde.

"Five.........oh damn!!!!!"

Clyde leaps over the front counter and does not move out of fright. "Way to go, Clyde! Captain America's scared of you!" James adds his insult from his own secure spot in an empty booth away from the action in the dining area.

"Shut up!"

Polly tries to flee from the action when part of her uniform is snagged to a window handle. Struggling to free herself, she hears Baby closing in on her entering the drive-through station. Brandon stands outside the fast-food restaurant with the rest of the shocked and stunned crowd. He strolls over a few feet to Angela. "Where's Polly?"

Angela shakes her head, "I thought she ran outside with us."

"Dang, I think she may be inside. I've got to help her!" Without hesitation, Brandon runs back inside. Bolting through the entrance doors, Brandon discovers Polly stuck in the drive-through station. Baby slithers a few feet away from her. Jumping over the front counter, he nearly steps on Clyde; his hands and feet shake in fright.

"Is that you, Clyde? Dang! Let a real hero take care of business." Brandon mocks him, running past Baby on its side courageously through the narrow space between him and the snake. He approaches Polly with an annoyed look on her face, continuing to struggle.

"Brandon! Thank you; now, please get me out of here!"

"Don't worry; I got this. I've always wanted to say that!"

Brandon pulls and tugs hard on Polly's uniform, trying to rip it loose. "Hurry, it's close!" She examines the distance between Baby and them. Her heart races fast, eyes on the verge of tears. "Don't worry, girl; I'll get this done!" Brandon pulls hard with his two strong hands ripping part of her snagged uniform, freeing her. She stands behind him with her hands in his back, admiring his courage. Baby slinks closer to them, now a couple of feet away. Baby stops, staying silent as it hears a familiar sound; the voice of its mistress.

"Baby!" Lynn shouts, and Baby responds, remaining still until Lynn takes her Boa in her hands, securing it in her grasp. "Now you know Mama can't take you anywhere if you can't stay in your cage." She chides her pet. An astonished Brandon and Polly take cautious steps towards Lynn. "I'm so sorry. I had started driving out of here, and I didn't notice Baby's cage wasn't locked until a few minutes ago. There was traffic on Figueroa and Exposition. That's why I took so long to come back. When I drove back and saw the crowd outside, I had a feeling Baby was on the loose. As I said, I'm very sorry. This won't happen again."

Clyde's shock wears off, regaining the air of confidence. "All right, so you're the one who's responsible for scaring away my employees, my customers, and me?"

Lynn faces Clyde and nervously shakes his hand. "Hello sir, uh, I just want to tell you that I'll repay for any damages my pet may have caused."

Clyde ends his façade of bravery long enough to admire her beauty. "Why, that's all right, miss. No harm is done." Clyde's loose lips reveal the news that he should have kept to himself until later. "The owner of this place is going to close it down in two weeks, so your little snake didn't do too much damage at all." Brandon and Polly glance at each other with puzzled looks. Clyde felt challenged on this matter by Brandon. "Two weeks? That's how long we have? Why didn't you tell us this when you showed up? Mr. Saeed told you this?"

Clyde backs away. "Oh yeah, we had a talk about it…"

"Does this mean we'll have to start looking for new jobs?" Polly crosses her arms over her body, not happy with this sudden revelation.

"Man Clyde, this ain't your day after all, ain't it player?" Brandon said mockingly.

"Now I know why I broke up with you." Polly pulls Brandon next to her. "Because it takes a man to tell us what's on the real. Sorry, but I'd rather be with someone like Brandon, not a "man" who couldn't help a woman in distress."

159

"Hey now," Clyde puts up his hands. "I had a moment of PTSD. I couldn't get over it."

"The only Post Traumatic Stress Disorder you're going to have Clyde, is when word of our little adventure gets out." Brandon sees the few customers with smartphones in their hands. "I can't wait to see you in action online."

Clyde puts up his hands. "Hey, hey." He shouts to the remaining customers, "I was just acting! I'm trying to get in the acting business, and the snake was only used as a comedy prop, for real!" He tries in vain to make himself look good, but Polly giggles.

"Oh no, it's not like that." She turns to the customers remaining and returning back. "He was definitely serious! That's how he is, chicken! A big ole coward! He's scared of a little…."

"Dang, girl!" Clyde disagrees with her. "You're bitter, so your opinion doesn't count!"

Clyde takes one look to his left and watches the customers start filing back in, including the ones who stayed taking pictures and recording all of the action which took place. Chances are it has already gone viral, exposing Clyde as one look at his social media account full of mock insults and taunts are posted. "Dang! This ain't nothing nice." He curses under his breath. Brandon holds Polly close to him, refusing to let go. Having already impressing her with his bravery, he takes one more brave action to secure her heart. "Would you like to go out with me sometime?" Polly smiles, nodding her head. "Of course! Sorry I wasted my time with Clyde. I know I won't do the same with you. You're handsome, brave, and I want to know you better."

"I like to do the same with you too." Brandon smiles, knowing he will get to work right away on sending his resume to the start-up multimedia company very soon.

160

Mr. Saeed bursts through the door. His face has a look of angst, bothered by the unwanted attention his establishment received on social media. "Where is Clyde? Where is he?"

"Mr. Saeed!" Brandon waves him over, joining the group of James, Angela, Francine, Polly, and Ivan. "We were just talking about you. So we have two weeks left. Is that right, sir?"

Saeed crosses his arms and nods. "Yes, I was hoping Clyde already told you. Look, I'll put in a good word for everyone because I have some good news for you all. I just finished a meeting with my family. It looks like we might have other projects lined up that we'll need experienced workers with data entry, call centers, anything that fits your specific skills."

Polly's face radiates with a bright smile. "Does that mean we'll still have jobs after we close here?"

"Not quite sure, but anything's possible," Saeed said, giving his outgoing employees hope although Brandon has a different plan in mind, one he intends to work out once his time as an employee at the Burger Palace is over. Saeed looks around for someone. "Excuse me, but has anyone seen Clyde?"

As for the romantic one himself, he shamelessly puts the move on Lynn outside by the door. Baby slithers in her hands. "I think you're a cutie. You're very lovely, and I would like to go out with you one night."

Lynn smiles with Baby in her arms. "No offense, but I don't know." She tells him in the hope of letting him down softly. "You probably don't like snakes, and my boyfriend won't approve of me talking with another man."

Dang, she's a challenge. Clyde figures out ways to gain the upper hand. Meanwhile, inside the Burger Palace, Brandon has a talk with Polly. "I liked what you said back there. It meant a lot."

"I'm just glad it's over between Clyde and me. He was so rude at times. He doesn't know that it's not about the height and muscles that make you a man, not at all. I have to tell you again, Brandon; you were brave back there. Thank you."

"Thank you." Brandon blushes. Then he starts to walk off, but Polly grabs him by his uniform lapels and rewards him with one long passionate kiss.

"I can pick you up around eight." She said. "One of many treats to come."

Brandon analyzes the passion behind the kiss, excited to see more of Polly later on. *Wow, I can't wait for those treats either.*

Clyde follows Lynn to her jeep believing in vain he could still convince her to leave her boyfriend. He pleads, "Come on, baby, I'm mad about you."

Lynn places a hand on her chest, believing he referred to her pet. "You're mad about Baby?"

"Yeah baby, I am. Come on, give it up."

"Okay, Baby's gonna give you a big kiss."

Anticipating a smack from Lynn, Clyde closes his eyes, puckers his lips, and kissed. However, he discovered what he kissed isn't human flesh.

It's reptilian.

"Arrrghhh, damn!!!!!" Clyde runs off screaming.

Francine and James, who witnessed everything, burst into uncontrollable laughter to the point of tears. "Know what, Francine?" James asks her.

"What?" Francine's eyes fill with water.

"Clyde should have said, 'do fries go with that snake?'"

"Ooooooo, help me!"

The Curse of The Green Paper

Hear the crackle of the green paper
it makes some famous, even few greater
the green paper brings attention
influence of the mind
carries with it power
pleasures over time.

The green paper stimulates
emotions to thrill
driving others to a frenzy
forcing them to kill
worshipping mammon that serves as a king
it becomes a lover
it satisfies everything.

It even helps carry on a tradition
habits of drug users
continuing their addiction
the green paper is used for both sides of the law
balancing good and evil
yes, the ultimate draw.

The green paper comes with a bloodstained cost
bearing the cries of young ones who lost
their lives for a goal, green paper to attain
what will it profit when nothing is to gain?

Of course, it is useful; lives it does save

opens doors for people
opportunities it paves
helping the hungry and even the homeless
giving low-income families a reason to feel
blessed.

In today's world, clearly, you can see
the green paper enslaves individuals
who don't want to be free
masses of citizens bow down
all a result of the lust of money; fatal disease.

The One Word I Never Thought...

Well, here we are
at the airport
your plane is boarding
about to depart
I just want to thank you
for being close one last time
before you forever leave my heart
our time is ended
things never worked out
like we planned
soon the grip
we have will loosen
as you share your love
with another man.

At this point in time
I must clear my throat
fight the tears swelling up
in my eyes
knowing that I will remember
your cute little smile
so bright and wide
there is just one word
I'd never thought I say
before I fade
from your mind
no longer will I be
your baby.

When you get on that plane
I pray your heart
will be filled
with joy, not tears
you have a good man now
he'll see you through
your doubts and fears
if you ever think about me
remember how
your heart was insecure
for so many years
then I made you believe again
in love for sure
it just didn't work out
for the both of us
but your new love
will treat you like a queen
that I do trust.

I know, I know
this is tough
for you as well
please, for me
don't you start to cry
this word I must tell
but this is the moment
I have to loosen my grip
and let you go
you'll always be special to me

I just wanted to let you know.

Now I must speak
gazing one last time
in your precious brown eyes
one word
how else can I say it?
Take care, my love
always and forever
Goodbye.

Transparent (Height)

I'm the new Invisible Man
under six feet
is where I stand
women don't want to see me
but yet yearn a man
God-fearing
possessing many qualities
they steadfastly refuse
denounce me for my height
but what if the same Creator
made my growth just right?

What if you refuse the clay
the Master purposely molds
to make your life better
don't wait until your journey gets old
for you to finally realize
here I stand before you
your Divine prize
but it's obviously apparent
the words I speak cannot
reach you
for I am, to you transparent.

Two Personas

Once I met a young woman
who's temperament
was compassionate
gentle and mild
little did I suspect
beneath her roamed
a spirit, freaky and wild
a persona that differed
from the ladylike nature
my eyes happened to view
in the true end
I was confounded
extremely confused.

She said she liked me
her attraction for me
was intense
before I knew it
she threw up
an emotional fence
so many cubits high
stretching out many yards wide
keeping me away
from her intimate mental side.

It's been years
since I saw her
it used to be

every now and again
the question lingers in my heart
were we destined to be lovers
or just occasional friends?
The reason I ask
is because I noticed
the other side
her alter ego
send out a call
for the man, she would like
catering to her in a special way
romance, it seems
doesn't belong in that flow.

To all you fellas out there
doing your best being gentlemen
listen and watch the message
your intended is trying to send
observe her closely
check out if it's reality or a fake
truth shall be revealed
if a union
between you both
is the best decision to make.

To you ladies reading this
now you understand
just a tad
why some of us who are men
cannot fully let go

it's difficult to deal
with two personas
a fair woman
and her alter ego
yes, we get hurt too
our emotions also get burned
now you claim
you want a man who's real
all we ask
is the same in return.

Seeking But Cannot Find

Every day I wake up
thankful that the sun
does rise
but I shake my head
when the truth hits me
in the face do I realize
the love of my life
gone, not there
another has her love and devotion
this is life, though it's not always fair.

This is part of what
we all go through
when the past
we curse and rue
losing a love tortures
claws at your mind
when we are so close
seeking but cannot find.

For example:
there was a woman
who cared for me
we were partners
shared everything
two lovers can indeed
then she went away

never did I see her again
when I last learned of her status
I had no chance with her again
even as a friend.

Catharsis
it's good for the soul
some say
for the time must come
to purge out your hurt
in a cleansing type of way
removing all fears
you may have
tearing away all doubts
learning from this lesson is hard
but that's what life is all about.

Music plays
four o'clock in the morning
the stillness of the hour
sunshine soon will be adorning
plants and waking up people
from late-night sleep
I write lyrics about a long lost love
which I never vow more to seek.

To all who read this
Cathartic
although it may be
we have lost someone

at one time or another
hoping they return
like a sailor lost at sea
time does heal all wounds
and if we're faithful shall
have our reward
but let the past be the past
and let's make the future bright
as we move forward.

Last Night at the Club

Progress has arrived in South Los Angeles. It isn't the progress that will build storefronts to elevate a community financially, but one in which the old replaces the new in the form of affordable housing for low-income citizens. Developers have converged on the Southside to build such residences, competing to see who can create a hub for those in need of a place to live. Local politicians feel this is the way to face a growing problem that has affected many major cities for decades. Los Angeles is also scheduled to hold the Olympic Games within the decade. A barrage of homeless people will not help the city's image at all.

Among the many left without homes is a Black gentleman wearing only dark-colored sweatpants and a button-down shirt with a tail hanging out under a long sleeve sweater. He is young with long hair and a beard that grows on his face. His appearance is not welcoming, his body odor repellent. The young man, who is known by the name Haynes struggles to get by poking his hand into trash cans to retrieve unfinished food, wandering in the front of a local convenience store with an outstretched hand in the hopes a polite soul will provide him whatever change they offer, riding city buses to get to one destination or another. At night, he searches for a decent place he can find a pleasant sleep. Whether it's on the top of concrete steps of a deserted church building or the many buildings scheduled for construction from the same developers building in the city. Haynes discovers one such vacant building in the area alongside a row of shut down or gated edifices. It has a human-sized wooden board covering the front entrance. Haynes turns to see the street behind him is quiet. There are

175

no police cars in the area to accost him if he is successful in entering this boarded-up storefront. Picking at the side of the board with his fingers, Haynes achieves success by prying open one side and very carefully slips inside what seems to be the interior of an abandoned restaurant. His nose has difficulty tolerating the dusty atmosphere surrounding him inside this abandoned space. His eyes observe decades of dust settled on vinyl seats next to long tables in between. A group of stairs leads up to an upper floor. The restaurant's wide space is filled with three rows of vinyl seats and tables in the middle. Quietly taking careful steps in the deserted dining room, Haynes tries to avoid decades of broken glass on the floor along with scattered debris. It is apparent to him he is not the only visitor to this site.

Haynes enjoys the quiet atmosphere the restaurant provides. He could tell it served ethnic food at one time, staring at an empty kitchen which served customers. Turning his head, he stretches out his short five-foot-five frame on the floor below. There is space ample enough surrounded by broken bottles and debris for him to lay down and take a nap on this late evening. He lays down thinking about how he fought for a country that has deserted him. Remembering the wars in a foreign country to punish "bad people," he returned home to a lonely hero's welcome at the airport. No crowd nor parades saluted him for his service. The Veterans Administration helps out with his hospital bills, but finding a place is hard to come by. Haynes's mother died when he was a young child. His relationship with the rest of his family is complicated at best. He is too prideful to ask for help in finding a place to live. For the moment, this space of a clean floor will suit his needs. He muses when the sun rises in the morning, he will be on his way to parts unknown, tired of asking people for money. All he wants to do is live like any other person desires. Resting his head on the floor, Haynes closes his eyes slowly and suddenly drifts away to the peaceful realm of sleep.

Slowly, Haynes wakes up dazed and confused. He was not in the middle of a dirty floor inside a deserted, boarded-up restaurant. He lifts his arms from the marble floor beneath him, rising to discover he is standing behind an empty bar full of customers. He finds his torn, raggedy clothes now transformed into a long sleeve shirt covering his arms with suspenders holding up a pair of pants. One glance into a mirror on the wall shocks Haynes now with a low-cut hairstyle and mustache on his face. The confused gentleman pats his stomach, feeling the fabric of a long sleeve shirt he now wears with a dark buttoned vest. An older, heavy-set man calls out to him as he mixes a drink for a well-dressed woman with a cigarette in her hand on the other side of the bar.

"Haynes! Haynes! Wake up!" The older man calls for him. His eyes grow wide with anger shouting at the gentleman who responds to his birth name. "Serve those two gents in front of you! What the hell were you lying on the floor anyway? This ain't no time to go to sleep?"

"I'm…. I'm sorry." Haynes lifts a hand to his face, still in his dazed state. He wonders how did he appear in this place, this very spot at this moment? One minute he sought to take refuge in a deserted building; the next…he is now standing behind a bar abuzz with customers ordering drinks in a place he doesn't recognize. The dress style, the abundance of Black people walking around in a relaxed state is a long way from where he was. He faces the older man with an open mouth, itching to find a reason for his appearance behind the wooden bar.

"I'm sorry, boss." Haynes quickly deducts who he is talking to. "I must have hit my head." The older man

177

reaches out with a hand and rubs his head with a towel. He shakes his head with a smirk taking a look at his younger counterpart. "Boy, you better watch yourself. This is a big night. We can't afford to be slackin'. You know Mr. Sullivan would have a big ole fit if he saw you there takin' a break! Satin Blue is on stage tonight. You know we always have a big crowd when she performs." The older man hands Haynes a bottle turning at the two Black men awaiting their drinks. They are well dressed in different colored pinstriped suits with fedoras on top of their heads matching their suits. Haynes surmises they must be rich, ready-made men. One of them with a complexion close to caramel nods at the older man. He sports a mustache; his demeanor expresses a severe attitude. "Don't worry about it. Make sure you get our drinks before Satin Blue starts singin'."

"No problem with that, sir. I'll make them for you." The older man begins to mix their drinks with ease as if he knew what they preferred. Haynes stands befuddled, watching the older man mix the drinks with relative ease. He spots Haynes standing next to him with a puzzled look. "What's the matter, boy? Ain't you seen my work on drinks before? You look like you're really out of it. How are you?"

"Sorry for asking, but who are you? Who's Mr. Sullivan?" Haynes questions him with a puzzled look on his face. After delivering the drinks to both men, the older man pulls Haynes to the side, wrapping an arm around him. "Oh boy, what happened to you? I guess that bottle hit you hard, didn't it?"

"What bottle?" Haynes looks around the bar, starting to get his bearings.

"The bottle you said sent you to the floor and knocked you out. That's what I think. You must have been mixing a drink with a bottle that got away from you. You recognize me, don't you? My name is Deke, short for Deacon. We've known each other for ten years after this hotel was built."

"Hotel?" Haynes lowers his brow. "We're in a hotel? I thought this is a bar!"

"It is." Deke nods his head. Hairs from his gray mustache fly in the air from him taking a breath. "This is Club Sullivan owned by Mr. Sullivan here on Central Avenue. It's named after him too. I thought you already knew that! Do you need a break, son? Do you need some time in the room to get yourself back together? Don't take too long. Satin Blue's going to be on stage in twenty minutes. I hear she has a hot act tonight. She told us not to miss it."

"Who is this Satin Blue?" Haynes asks. His confusion begins to clear, but he wants to know the answer to his recent question.

"Boy, you sure are confused! Satin Blue is our lead entertainer. She performs every Tuesday night here at the hotel. That young girl has a sweet voice, whew! I'm surprised you don't know who she is. That bottle must have hit you harder than I thought."

Haynes raises his arms in the air. "No, no, I'm fine. I will take your suggestion and rest for a while. I will be back, believe me."

"Take five. I need you to come back before she starts performin'. Don't be late!"

"I won't. Thanks, Deke." Haynes paces his steps slowly. Consciousness and the proper use of his feet gradually return to his addled mind. His eyes scan the club patrons around him. They are dressed in the finest suits for men, dresses for women. Haynes doesn't even know where his break room is, but his eyes did follow a sign leading him to an unused space in the hotel's rear. He nods to a couple with glee on their faces passing him by. With a couple of steps inside the empty room, Haynes admires

179

how clean it is. A coat hangs on the back of a chair, which he sits in with no problem. A printed object his elders once called a newspaper lays on the floor. He stares at a masthead with the newspaper's name he does not recognize to look at the date. His eyes could not believe the date on which this was published. Haynes's body froze, hands shaking in surprise reading the year. According to what he has seen, Haynes speculates he is in the mid-1920s based on the style of clothing his grandfather showed him in one of those old magazines his elder kept when he was a young boy. Dropping the newspaper on the wooden floor, Haynes shakes his head, unaccepting of where he is and the date on which he is placed. He realizes he's still in South Los Angeles, but wasn't this the same run-down building he took refuge in? Is he dreaming, or has he been transported to this date for some unknown reason? The weight of the realization from his newfound discovery almost causes him to crumple into tears. Haynes decides it is a dream and to make the most out of it as best he can.

In another part of the city, two cars, Bel-Air Chevrolets with bright headlights, shine in the middle of a deserted field without lights near the Baldwin Hills dam. Doors open, a tall Negro over six feet tall with a suit to fit his lean frame steps out, dragging a shorter Black man with hands tied behind his back begging for mercy. From one car's back seat emerges a strikingly young and imposing Negro male with a butter pecan complexion in his late twenties, standing a little over six feet. He is surrounded by several other well-dressed Negroes who circle around the helpless man who appears to be in his fifties with a stout figure. His hairline recedes to the point of near baldness. He continues to scream and scream until the well-dressed Negro plants a backhanded slap to the man's face sending him to the dirt below. Sticking a toothpick in his mouth, the well-dressed Negro bends over his intended victim, struggling to break

180

free from the bonds tied behind him. Laughing out loud, the rest of his boys laugh along with him, mocking the victim on the ground. He nods to the taller man, who keeps a handgun pointed at the gentleman.

"Now you see Ricky; when I say I want my money, I don't play around. You know ole Dallas Red don't play. I'm going to ask you one last time before you die. Where's my money?"

"Red! Red! Oh Red, please don't kill me! I promise I'll have it before Friday! Please don't kill me!"

"I hate it when one of my people beg me for their life," Red says, teeth firmly on the toothpick. "I also get turned on seeing a wimp like you beg me to keep you alive. Unfortunately, I don't have much time. As you can tell, my boys and I are wanted men. I hoped to hear you say you had it ready for me now. I guess not. Stretch."

With one nod, the taller Negro Stretch pulls the trigger of his handgun with confidence. The sound of a single shot silencing the older Ricky was music to Red's ears. He knew Ricky couldn't come up with the money he sought, but he knew of one person who does.

"Red! Ricky told me he works as a cook for a club in some hotel down on Central Avenue. He says he knows someone named uh, Deke. Should we take a visit to this club and see him?" One of Red's men addresses him.

"That wouldn't be the Club Sullivan, would it? You know, I've always wanted to check it out. I heard they have a sweet girl named Satin Blue who sings there. You do know what they say about blue and red going together?" Red laughs, as does the rest of his men. With a quick gesture of a hand wave, they jump back in their cars and depart towards their next destination Club Sullivan. Ricky's body is the only one back in the deserted area where it serves as a reminder to cross Dallas Red means your unfortunate end.

Holding a cigar in one hand, a barely well-dressed man with a pecan complexion enters the bar with a confident look speaking to two equally well-dressed broad-shouldered men beside him. He stands tall at five foot nine inches surrounded by other men wearing the same pinstripe suit as he. The young gentleman appears as if he returned from gambling and an evening with the rest of his men who surround him. Deke nods his head at him, tapping Haynes on the arm to acknowledge their new visitor. "That's Mr. Sullivan's son, Jimmy. Why don't you wave to him?"

Haynes did, and in no time, Jimmy approaches them with a confident stroll towards them, still retaining the cigar in one hand. "Deke, how are things going for our big night?" Haynes hears the words come out of Sullivan's mouth. He sounds educated, as if he graduated from those affluent white schools in the city. Sullivan is a graduate from one of the historically Black colleges in the South, although he is a native in this area of the city. He observes the smooth tongue-speaking words he has heard before but never in the manner Jimmy uses them. He forces a smile as Jimmy looks in his direction with an outstretched hand. "Mr. Haynes, it's a pleasure to see you again. I know you must be ready for our headliner tonight. That Satin Blue is quite an attractive woman, isn't she?"

Haynes accepts his hand, shaking it in return. He feels compelled to answer Jimmy, which he does by way of a slight smile and nod. "Yes, yes, I guess so." He says although he has never met this woman Sullivan refers to. Suddenly, Jimmy's mood changes. He maintains his grip on Haynes's hand a bit tighter than usual. With a cold stare into his eyes, Haynes hears this message from Sullivan. His voice lowers along with the intense gaze. "I know you're sweet on the girl. You have every right to be, but she's also family. I suggest you watch yourself if you plan on being her man. I'll be watching you." Haynes feels the release of

182

the tight grip from his hand. Sullivan turns around to play the role of happy owner, although Haynes knows better now. Confused, he shakes his head, wondering how he could treat a woman he's never met? Scratching the side of his head, he looks at the bar. The frenetic activity is slowed down, awaiting the arrival of the woman everyone's waiting for, Satin Blue.

Deke is at the far end of the bar, speaking into a wall phone. His facial expressions display a sense of dread and anger. Haynes hears him shouting on the other end, hearing the words, "If he shows his face around here, he'll regret it!" before turning away to wash out a couple of glasses in a small sink in the bar area. The crowd grows as anticipation sets in. Haynes examines the audience sitting at round tables in the club with professional men in suits sitting with their paramours, significant others, or their wives. He notices a few men taking puffs on their cigarettes, engaging in loud conversation with the women sitting near their tables. The small stage area is dim except for a lone spotlight shining in the center. Lingering in his mind is Jimmy's warning to him. Questions fill his head for the reason of his involvement with the young woman, and to what extent? Perhaps they will be answered soon as Haynes washes out the last of the glasses to hear a loud noise stir near the front entrance. His eyes look in that direction of the stunning Negro woman covered in a fur coat. She extends an arm waving at the crowd, ready for her performance. Youthful with the most beautiful smile on her face, she walks with two of Jimmy's men towards the dressing room in the back of the club. Haynes couldn't take her eyes off her alluring shape hidden under a velvet dress. Her hair is fixed upwards with a bun holding it in place. Gently, she reaches an older man sitting in his seat extending his hand for her to shake it, which she gladly accepts. Passing by the bar, her captivating black eyes lock

183

on Haynes. His eyes return the gaze for a reason. She blows a kiss right at him, disappearing into the dressing room. Deke slaps him on the shoulder, laughing. It appears whatever upset him a minute ago no longer does. He bends over with a hearty smile on his face.

"She got you sprung good, huh?"

"Was that her? Was that…Satin Blue?"

"Boy, don't you know your lady? Of course, that was her! Listen, I saw you and Jimmy huddled a few minutes ago. Whatever he told you, you don't have to worry. She likes you, and I know you like her. Don't let him ruin this chance for love."

Haynes wanted to ask why he would be infatuated with her, but he couldn't. He still doesn't know why he is in a nightclub inside a hotel in this period and time. He takes a step back and feels the wooded edge of the bar. It is real. Like everything else he's experienced so far, it is all too real. The smoke-filled air, the clanging of glasses, the boisterous discussions among patrons. Even Jimmy's handshake and exchange with him. He tries not to accept what he has seen and heard, but he realizes it is as real as standing behind a bar. It wasn't too long ago that he walked as a lonely homeless man in the city who decided to rest. Now he finds himself fully dressed in a place unknown to him, experiencing feelings for a woman he's never met. It is a sensation he couldn't understand or figure out.

As the night continues, Haynes could not get Satin Blue out of his mind. He felt like approaching her in the dressing room to ask a few questions, but the patrons' orders kept flowing in, preparing for her act. Deke had an unusual spring in his step, bouncing up and down the bar, speaking with the kitchen's cook, and at times glance at the front entrance nervously. Haynes wonders why that would be so. Deke approaches him with a broad slap to his back. He smiles, flashing his crooked bottom teeth and curled-up mustache. Placing his arm around him, Haynes feels a bit disturbed by his gesture. "Lucky you boy. Look at them drinks sitting up on the bar." Haynes observes on the bar counter two bottles of vodka standing on top of a tray. Squinting his eyes, Haynes turns at Deke, wondering what this was all about.

"Blue just placed that order. She asked for you to see her in the dressing room."

"She wants me to take this to her?" Haynes asked. The question causes Deke to back up a step, caught off guard. "Of course, boy! She's *your* woman, ain't she? Now go ahead and take those to her." Haynes lifts the tray over his right shoulder with unexpected skill and walks carefully towards Satin's dressing room. He shakes his head with the realization he was going to talk to her alone at last. With a hard rap on the door with his left hand, Haynes watches the door open, revealing Blue smiling at him with a gentle stare in her eyes. Her pecan complexion shines when a sliver of moonlight hits it. "Lay them down over there." She points to a small table in the corner of the room. He fails to notice Blue dressed in only a towel covering her body but accentuating her lovely form in his nervousness. She greets him with open arms, gently wrapping them around him. Leaning forward, she plants a kiss on his cheek. Haynes is still quite curious about how they met, but the romantic gesture he experiences is something he enjoys very much.

"Thank you, Blue." Automatically, Haynes knows what to call the smiling young woman who proceeds to loosen her towel, revealing a naked body. Haynes's eyes widen, his manhood stiffens, watching a pair of bare breasts jiggle up and down as Blue takes a casual stroll across the room to slip on a bra sitting on a chair and a dark blue dress for the upcoming performance.

"What's the matter, baby? You've seen me without clothes plenty of times. You even sucked on my big ole breasts last night." Blue swerves her head, so her cheeks meet his.

"Wait a minute; I did what?" Haynes's jaw dropped. He now understands his relationship with Blue was more than casual. It was sexually passionate. There's nothing wrong with her, Haynes surmises watching the young woman slip on her dress which hugs each and every curve of her body. He is captivated by her hairstyle. It is different than the weaves the women who pass him by on the street wear. Blue's hair is fashioned in what she calls a Josephine Baker look. Haynes scratches his head, trying to figure out who is this "Josephine Baker," but he listens to Blue telling him how she first laid eyes on him working at the bar. She explains that she knew he works for her uncle, Mr. Sullivan, but she had to know him because she feels he is the one for her. She admits how she had pursued him as a young girl knowing that it was a man's job to chase after a woman they adored as Blue was a senior in a nearby college when they met. Haynes stands up against a wall as she tells her whole story; a local girl raised by a pair of well-to-do parents who left Allensworth, moving back to Los Angeles to establish and operate the same hotel and club her uncle now owns. Blue could have gone overseas to Paris like her idol, Ms. Baker but decided to stay in the States and sing in local clubs starting with her uncle's.

"Aw shoot! I go on stage in twenty minutes! Haynes, I want you to know that you're my man, and I love you very much. I'm waiting for you to pop that question so you and I can be together forever." Blue wraps her loving arms around him, whispering in his ear. Haynes once again feels his manhood stirring and stiffening, growing harder each second. Her breasts press against his chest. Haynes feels compelled to kiss her, which he does. His tongue locks with hers passionately. Haynes is now caught in a web of lovemaking Blue spun to perfection. He didn't want to

186

escape as she…. causes him to sink deeper in this web. Hard raps on the door cause this brief reunion to end abruptly.

"Blue! Blue!" The unmistakable sound of Jimmy's voice is heard behind the door. "Fifteen minutes till showtime! Get ready, girl!"

"Damn." Blue huffs in frustration, desiring to spend more time with her man. "My cousin's right. I have to finish dressing for my set. I swear, I need a manager or assistant one of these days. I hope that once I make the big time, I will." Reaching out with a hand, Blue touches Haynes about to step out the door. "The drinks were an excuse to see you. If all goes well, we should have a little time to ourselves later. Perhaps you would like to join me for a drink so we can continue our lovin'?"

"Yeah, yeah, I would love that." Haynes nods his head empathically. The lovers wave goodbye to each other. Haynes steps under the doorway headed back to the bar. Jimmy suddenly meets him at the stairwell. He doesn't look pleased with all.

"You couldn't keep your hands off her, huh? You just had to see her."

"Mr. Sullivan, sir, I didn't mean to. It's just……."

Jimmy nods with a sinister smile on his face. "Ah, it seems you and Deke are in cahoots with each other. He told me Satin placed an order for a couple of drinks which you had no trouble carrying up to her dressing room. Had I not knocked on the door, that dressing room would be smelling full of sex right now!"

"Mr. Sullivan, please," Haynes begs. "I meant no harm. She did place the order, and I……" Jimmy couldn't hold it in much longer. He explodes in laughter which confuses a surprised Haynes.

"You think I'm going to fire you, son? Listen, I know all about you and my cousin from the very beginning. She

187

even told me how much she digs you. It must be because you're a handsome young man with a lot going on for yourself. I'll tell you this; after tonight, whatever happens between you two is none of my business. I've always looked out for that girl, so now she deserves someone who will take over my job. I hope it's you. I've been hard on you, but that's because I think she's going places, and I want someone she loves to go with her. Do you understand me, my friend?"

"I think so, Mr. Sullivan." Still confused, Haynes nods. "Excuse me, sir; I have to return to the bar. I think Deke is missing me."

"I gave him a five-minute break. He claims to have an emergency back at his home, so I told him to check into it. The both of you are okay right now. Everyone's ready for Blue to perform tonight."

With the knowledge he will not be in trouble, Haynes nods once more, passing Jimmy on his way to the bar. Before he completely passes him, Jimmy takes Haynes by the arm to glance directly into his eyes with one final statement. "Now, if you don't treat her right, let's just say that I won't be a happy man. Her happiness means everything to me. If I catch you mistreating her in any way like beatin' or cheatin', you will regret the day you do. Understand me?"

"Yes, I do, Mr. Sullivan. Yes, I do."

"Good." Jimmy smiles satisfied with the answer. "Take your break too. You deserve it."

The lights are focused on a three-legged stool behind a microphone—a house bandstand in the back, almost invisible to the crowd. Patrons watching the elevated three-foot stage from their seats relax under cover of faint darkness. For some reason, Haynes's heart leaps while periodically manning the bar. Deke returns from his break, joining him. His eyes feel a pang of hunger for Blue's presence, his mind feeling it's funny he has feelings for a woman he's never met in a place and time unknown to him. He hears the clicking of heels in the back of the stage at the same time Jimmy walks up to the stage, taking the microphone in his hand to introduce his guest for the evening. Jimmy's light-colored suit shines under the lights, almost angelic in his appearance. Without hesitation, he makes his announcement to the audience.

"Welcome ladies and gentlemen to Club Sullivan. We are pleased and honored that you are our guests for this splendid evening. Our musical guest tonight is an accomplished performer. Her appearance at the Apollo Theatre in Harlem last week brought the house down! What can I say? She's an emerging star and well on her way to greatness. The fact she's my favorite cousin only makes me smile even brighter! As a reminder, if you are thirsty, please help yourself by visiting our bar located on the left side of the stage. Now for your enjoyment, here she is, the one and only Satin Blue!"

Hearing the loud ovation as she enters the stage, Blue flashes a broad smile observing the packed audience facing her. As her cousin revealed, she did perform in the famous Apollo Theatre in New York City's Harlem, playing to a much larger crowd. Blue is used to them by now overflowing just to hear her sing. To relieve her nervousness, she takes a seat on the small stool her cousin provided for her while she explains her progress as a singer. Haynes leans over the edge of the bar's counter to take a good look at her. Radiant in her dress, Blue takes the microphone in her hand to begin singing her song. The house band performs their set matching in rhythm with Blue's heavenly voice as she voices the lyrics of a certain love song. Haynes feels his heart surrendering to her now. The more he hears her, the deeper he falls for her. He shakes his head in a state of disbelief, knowing she feels a passion for him to the point she desires to be his wife. As a trickle of patrons slowly walk up to the bar, Haynes is engaged in taking their orders. He listens to Blue sing a song of love between requests, almost as if it were meant for him. It was.

Dallas Red and the rest of his men enter the club looking at the stage, observing Blue as a wolf to a lamb. With a quick swerve of his head, he directs his men to stand up against a wall in the back—Jimmy from his perch on the second floor where the dressing rooms are located spots Red. Gesturing to one of his men dressed in a black overcoat wearing a black hat, he whispers to his associate to keep a lookout. He has quite a reputation in this part of town. Red takes a puff of a cigarette he holds between his fingers, whispering to one of his men how "fine" Blue looks telling him, "I've got to make that woman mine. They say blue and red don't go together, but I can make it work. I have the tool to do it too." Red refers to his manhood as the "tool" he needs to make a connection with Blue.

Blue hears the overwhelming positive applause from a crowd shrouded in darkness. Flashing a bright smile, she soaks in the applause with a polite nod to them. Haynes claps empathically, flashing his smile. He takes in a deep breath anticipating his time with her after she is done for the evening. She immediately begins to sing another song in the same slow melodic tone the band plays. Jimmy walks up to the bar with his giant associate behind him, gesturing wildly with his hands to summon Deke and Haynes to greet him.

"This is my man Digger. Don't ask me why I call him that. Listen, we have a "guest" tonight. As a businessman, I have to make sure there's no trouble in this club. That's why I don't mess with folks. They don't mess with me. I

190

will say that gentleman standing against the wall in the back is a known felon and full of trouble." Jimmy nods towards Red's direction. "Let him or his posse back there order what they want. If there's any trouble, just let Digger know, and he'll take care of it."

Digger leans over the bar. His eyes are cold, staring directly at Deke and Haynes, who feel the chill looking back at him. "Ain't nothing to worry bout. I heard about this cat. If he starts trouble, he is out. No trouble. Let me know." Haynes hears the country accent in his voice. He sounds as if he is from the deep South but couldn't quite pin down the location. Watching Digger turn his back away from them to leave the bar, Haynes replies, "Funny; Digger looks like a bad man. I don't want to mess with him at all."

"Nah man, he's a cool cat." Deke fills a glass for a customer who patiently sits at the bar waiting for a drink. "Now you know why ole' Satin girl got you so sprung, huh?"

"She's very beautiful, no doubt. Say, do you think that fella Mr. Sullivan told us to look out for will show up here?"

"Most definitely. Maybe you never heard of Dallas Red, but I have. Fella is full of trouble. Best keep your eyes off him. He can sniff you out like a bloodhound to a wounded cat. He's a problem."

"What do you know about him?" Haynes fetches a bottle of vodka from a bottom shelf on the opposite wall to the bar.

"Besides his name? A young man showed up here from Texas a year ago, and all of the Central Avenue bar owners put a warning out for each other to watch out for him. He's been involved in some pretty shady stuff if you ask me: drugs and all other thangs. I wouldn't be surprised to know he's a pimp. He runs the businesses you and I don't want to get involved in." Just as Haynes listens to

191

Deke's warning, Red catcalls Blue on the stage, causing her to feel uncomfortable. "He's fresh too." Haynes feels angry for some reason. He does not appreciate the rudeness of Red. If he could, he would walk up to Red and let him know how he doesn't like the vulgar suggestions he is making to a woman who he doesn't know that well but feels a passionate attraction to. As he shakes his head back to reality, Haynes could only focus on serving the next drink while hearing Blue regain her composure to finish her song.

Red walks up to the bar keeping a lustful eye on Blue, fiddling with a gold watch in his hand. Haynes tenses up prepared to endure whatever words come out of Red's mouth. "Give me a glass of whiskey, please." Red issues his demand at Haynes, who stares into the green pupils of his eyes. Nervous, he begins serving his drink while keeping his eyes on Red, tapping on the bar with his fingers uttering profane comments towards Blue. "Look at that girl! I'd love to lay next to her and suck those…." Haynes presents his drink to Red. "Here you go, sir." Red cuts his comment short taking the drink in hand. Raising the glass, he takes a sip then wipes the moisture from his lips. "Damn! That's good! Say, you must be new. I ain't never seen you here before. Where you from?" Red nearly leans to the edge of the bar. Before Haynes could part his lips, Deke taps him on the shoulder, gesturing to follow him to the other side of the bar. Red smiles, laughing maniacally. "All right then, youngin'." He raises his glass in the air, still seated at the bar.

"You don't have to carry on talking with him. He'll get you in trouble, or worse." Deke says to Haynes, keeping his eyes on Red. "I know Deke. I just don't like the way he's looking at Blue."

"Nobody likes it." Deke shrugs. "Tell you what; Mr. Sullivan told us everything would have been taken care of.

All we have to do is act cool and serve these folks. I would also tell you not to talk with Red for too long. All he's trying to do is to get you to fight."

Jimmy interjects himself between his two bartenders. "Great night, isn't it?"

"Better than we thought, sir." Deke continues, wiping off moisture from his shirt. "I was just telling Haynes to be careful with Red. He asked Haynes where he's from. Already trying to start trouble, and he's not even drunk yet."

"We have a bigger problem than that, Deke. Bigger than Red's presence here tonight."

"What's the matter, Mr. Sullivan?" Haynes leans over to hear the bad news.

"I'm surprised my cousin didn't tell you. Oh well, it doesn't matter. I'm glad she's on the stage tonight. It could be her last time."

Deke's eyes widen. "What do you mean by that, sir?"

Jimmy lowers the crown of his hat, speaking in a hushed tone. "You two boys see what's happening at that Dunbar Hotel a few blocks from here?"

"Ain't that the Hotel Somerville?" Deke says. "I heard they changed their name last year."

"Absolutely the same place." Jimmy nods. "One of my boys tell me they're getting quite the crowd over there. They have jazz every night while I had to almost fall on my knees to find this band for Blue. Now tonight is a wonderful night, a glorious evening. I fear it might be too little, too late."

"What do you mean by that, Mr. Sullivan?" Haynes's eyes also widen.

"We own the building, but the land......that's another story. A white man living in the hills gave this to my family at a good price, provided we keep bringing in enough customers to satisfy our rent. The good news is if we keep

193

having crowds like tonight, we'll be just fine. The bad news is our family can't continue to sink money into this club if we're not making a profit without a large crowd. Blue's the only one who keeps packing them in, but when you look at the Dunbar and that they have a club in the hotel…let's just say you gentlemen need to look for more bars to work in soon. This could be one of our last nights."

The bombshell sinks deep into the hearts of Haynes and Deke, outraged not being told sooner. "Mr. Sullivan, that's not right! You should have told us! How were we supposed to know?"

"Sorry, Deke, but I have put in a good word to a few associates of mine who own clubs downtown. The funny thing is, I've been told there's some bad news coming out from the East coast. Bankers and all committing suicide now that stocks everywhere are going down, even mine."

"What happens now, Mr. Sullivan?" Haynes asks. "Will we get paid tonight?"

"Yes. Yes, you will." He nods. "I made sure you two will be paid tonight along with the cooks in the kitchen, the band, my cousin….everyone will get paid for the evening, and if the crowds keep coming in, we might hold on just a little bit longer. Still, what I was told about the stocks going down, there might be bad news coming our way."

"What about Blue? I'm happy she's going to be paid, but what happens after that?"

"That's a question only you can answer, Mr. Haynes." Jimmy stares him right in the eyes. "There's no doubt you two will be married. If not soon, then it will happen at some point. I'll make sure both of you will have a roof over your heads to start. Then it's up to you two to live your lives as you see fit. Deke, I won't forget you. I'll make sure you'll be taken care of well."

Jimmy spots Digger waving a massive arm in the air, beckoning him to come. "Gentlemen, sorry to bring you the bad news. We'll talk later."

Watching Jimmy walk away from the bar, Haynes resumes his duties, greeting customers while serving drinks. Despite all that was said, there is a feeling of security he hasn't felt in a while. He faintly remembers his old life begging passers-by for change to buy food or drink. He also recalls entering through the open doors of gas station restrooms to relieve himself. It all comes back to him of the existence he lived before he woke up in the club. He smiles, knowing he has a job, a good one, and his coworkers and boss are friendly towards him. Haynes captures a thought in his head he does not care how he ended up in this place. He knows if he can help it, he never wants to leave. This is the life he's always wanted.

Blue parts her lips with the closing lyrics of her last song. Closing her eyes as she mouths the words of the sweet melodious tones, she releases out towards the audience shrouded in shadow; the young songstress slowly lowers her head as motioning a bow towards them. Raising her head slowly, her eyes flicker with a wide smile on her face adorning the inspiring applause and cheer from the same audience she now sees fully with the overhead lights above resuming their illuminance. Instinctively, she raises a hand waving towards the cheering audience in front of her. She turns towards the bar and plants a kiss by placing her hands to her lips, sending it to Haynes, who joins the audience and Deke in applause. Red and his two men also joined in the applause, although his eyes focus on the recipient of the kiss standing behind the bar.

"Must be her man." One of Red's men leans over to whisper in his boss's ear.

"Won't be for long." Red vows.

195

Watching Red from a four-foot pub table in a corner adjacent to the bar and kitchen, Digger sits slowly sipping a drink keeping his eyes on Red and his men. He awaits the moment to act. He hopes it won't come down to a confrontation with the huge man next to Red leaning against a wall. If it has to come to that, he will not hesitate. He hopes it won't come down to gunplay which he is an expert. The war in Europe trained him for what he does for a living now. Digger has always been an expert in using a gun and taking a direct aim towards anyone he considers a target. Jimmy's brother was his fellow soldier-in-arms as they fought along the lines in France and other places just to survive. Since the war, Digger knows survival on the streets is just as bad as fighting a war. The winners regret their victories.

Blue steps down from the stage, waving Haynes over. Sullivan nods his head, approving the meet. Out of instinct or perhaps a growing attraction, Haynes takes Blue's outstretched hands, watching her flash a bright smile. "I want to tell the world! I want to let them know you're my man!" Blue says out loud.

"Are you sure?" Haynes smiles, very surprised but honored at her gesture.

"Yes! I do; I want to let them know!"

Taking the microphone, Blue turns to the audience to make the following announcement. "Ladies and gentlemen, I would like to introduce my fiancée, who you may have seen working behind the bar. My man, Mr. Haynes!" He hears the favorable applause from the crowd, laughing and smiling as he holds Blue in his arm. He couldn't believe this moment. It is a dream he never wants to end. Wherever and how he arrived doesn't matter as long as he never wakes up or leaves this place; who knows how he appeared in this club holding a future wife while holding down a good job? He didn't care as he plants a kiss on Blue's lips for the audience to see. Red on the other hand…….

"Looks like we might have to visit Lover Boy before tonight's over. That Blue is a fine woman. No way should she waste her time with that sucker."

"What are you going to do, Red?" The large man beside him asks. "We can't make a move now. Too many people."

Red lowers his hat while waving a hand in the air. "Naw, we're not going to make our move now. Let's just wait until the club shuts down for the night. We have time on our side plus, I can't wait until I get a little touch of Satin Blue. That girl is going to be mine tonight!"

Two hours after the patrons left several tips enjoying their time at the club, Blue finishes dressing, hearing the raps outside her door. Haynes smiles as she opens the door, equally happy to see him there. She greets him in a form-fitting outfit that accentuates her curves. "You were great!" Haynes lowers his head, continuing to smile. "You sound nice. I love your voice."

"Silly boy!" Blue taps his arms playfully. "You look like a sick puppy dog standing out there. Come in." She moves out of Haynes's path, allowing him to enter the room. Haynes sees the dress she wore on stage spread out on one chair next to a table and the vodka bottles she ordered ready to be opened.

"Would you like to join me?" She asks with a smile on her face gesturing to the unopened bottles on the table.

"You sure?" Haynes feels his throat tighten. A drink at this point would be nice. He knows what might happen, but he isn't concerned. He longs for her touch, a chance to hold her in his arms. He quickly steps in front of her, taking a bottle in one hand, slowly opening it. He nods his head with a broad smile of his own. "Forget my last question.

197

Yes, I would like to have a drink with you." Haynes joins her in a toast to her success, slowly pouring the intoxicating liquid into two drinking glasses on the table next to the vodka. He wishes it would be more than just a simple drink he shares with her.

They sit facing each other behind the small round table in her dressing room. They sip slowly with laughter and smiles on each of their faces. Haynes attempts to break the ice by repeating his glowing praise of her performance on stage. "You were outstanding tonight."

"Anytime I hear that from you is always nice to hear." She leans forward then reclines back in her chair. "I appreciate Jimmy offering me this opportunity. I know the rest of the family will be glad to hear that I was a headliner at his club, but I have to be honest with you. Please don't tell Jimmy this, but I would love to sing at the Dunbar. My girlfriends spent a night there, and they tell me you see all the movie stars, intellectuals, everybody who's somebody goes there. And the jazz! Wow, they told me the bands they have playing at the hotel are the best in the country! Not meaning any offense to the young men who played my set tonight, but the Dunbar would be a great place for me to be seen!"

"I'm sure Jimmy doesn't want to hear that."

"I know he's family and Haynes; I appreciate all he's done for me. He's my favorite cousin and all, but I have to look out for him. You understand, right? I had to cancel an opportunity in Paris so that I could help Jimmy tonight. Don't get me wrong; I love my cousin, and I love Club Sullivan, I do." Blue stretches out her hands, pleading to Haynes he doesn't get the wrong idea about her. He shakes his head, assuring her thoughts didn't offend him. "The way I see it Blue, the family does come first, but you're young, and there's a whole world out there for you to take advantage of. I don't see you having a problem with having

198

big dreams, bigger than Club Sullivan. Jimmy will find a way to keep this place running, or at least I hope so."

Blue rises from her seat to fall into Haynes's lap, still holding a glass of vodka in her hand. "Thank you! I didn't want to sound selfish. I just wanted you to know I have dreams, big dreams outside this place. I just want them to come true."

"Blue, they will. Just keep it up with that fine voice of yours."

"I sure will, baby."

The two lovers continue to kiss and sip away into the night. Haynes feels the gentle pressing of her lips into his. He enjoys her company as she does his. The vodka's intoxicating effect already provides a carnal suggestion that prompts him to remove his shirt, and who knows what else?

Deke heaves two trash bags in the air to place them in a huge trash container in the rear. Passing through the door, his eyes detect one of Red's men leaning against a brick wall near the trash container. He seems calm as he witnesses the gentleman with a cocoa butter complexion whip out a cigarette from his jacket pocket and lights a match to smoke it. Deke continues to empty the trash inside the five-foot container acting as if the stranger isn't there.

"Great night, wasn't it?" The stranger asks Deke, who slowly nods his head. "Yeah, yeah, it was."

"That girl who just sang, Blue. She doesn't have a man, does she?"

"I believe that ain't none of my business." Deke didn't want the stranger to know his knowledge of the relationship between Haynes and her.

"But up on that stage, she just admitted that young man serving with you at the bar is her man."

"They might be together, but again it's none of my business."

"I see." The stranger reaches down into his suit jacket. Deke hurries to go back inside. He hears a voice ordering him to stop. "Hold it, my simple country friend." The stranger holds a handgun in the air, barking at Deke to approach him. "I only asked because my man Dallas Red plans to make her his woman tonight. A fine piece of ass like hers is just right for him, don't you think?"

Deke scans his eyes to the right. He hopes the stranger doesn't notice the two-foot circular trash can behind him. If he could only turn and throw it at the stranger, he might have a chance. The stranger coughs. He lifts his left hand, holding the gun in his right. Deke quickly turns to throw the trash can towards the stranger who ducks and, with one release of the trigger, shoots at Deke, who falls to the ground as his back was turned. Vapor from the fateful shot rises in the cold night air. A minute passes for the stranger who creeps closer to his victim to see his aim hits Deke squarely in the back, causing him unable to move. His life is fading by the minute, Deke's eyes begin to tear up. He knew he isn't long for this world. Soon he will either join the angels in the sky or the demons beneath the earth.

With his fading breath, Deke cries out, "Mama, please tell Father God to forgive me for all I've done! I don't want to die. Mama, I love you. I don't want to......"

Deke's eyes close for the last time. The stranger stands over him for a minute, feeling no remorse but determined to finish the job. He hopes the gunshot didn't alarm anyone passing through the club or anyone inside who might have heard it. He stuffs his weapon inside his suit jacket to open the door and enter inside, joining Red and his other assistant to help.

Haynes hears the shot rising from the floor, shirtless. "What was that?" His eyes bulge, turning right at Blue, covering herself just as Haynes zips up his pants and buttoning up his shirt.

"Baby! Did you hear that? What's going on?" Blue whispers in a panic.

"Shhhh!" Haynes places a finger between his lips to calm her down. He holds her hand to walk down the stairs quietly. They hear voices from Jimmy's office two doors down. Red and his other henchman, the taller gentleman, are inside. Red holds a handgun at Jimmy threatening him to open a safe in the wall behind his desk or shoot. Defiant, Jimmy shakes his head, refusing to open it. "I'm not going to be intimidated by a no-good hoodlum and his army of thugs!" He shouts from behind his desk.

"Fool! Don't you know who I am?" Red creeps closer to the desk, maintaining his aim. "I killed dummies with more swagger and fewer pennies than you! Dumb nigger, I am known all over! When they hear the name Dallas Red, people jump! Look at you, rich stuck up Negro! You think you tough, but you just like everyone else. You're only tough until you have a bullet up your ass! Now open that damn safe, or else I start blasting your Black hide!"

Blue and Haynes stand right outside the door next to the dining area full of chairs surrounding the round tables draped in a white cloth. Blue holds a hand to her mouth, trying to keep herself from going insane. Haynes wants to pass the open doorway and escape with Blue out the front. Their ears perk up when they hear two gunshots in the back. A loud groan follows, which Haynes interprets as an ominous sign of their predicament. Digger emerges through the back door with a nod towards Blue and Haynes, having dispatched Deke's killer with his handgun. A vaporous trail floats in the air only to disappear. The shots capture the attention of Red's taller henchman stepping outside the door. He discovers no one in the dining area. Digger stands in front of a door leading to the men's restroom in the

201

club's rear. Blue and Haynes duck under one table next to the walkway where the taller henchman tiptoes carefully, weapon extended for a quick shot. Digger suddenly reveals himself out into the open, firing a shot. The taller henchman does the same. Within seconds, there is silence. Blue and Haynes rise from under the table to see both men on the floor.

"Oh no!" Blue yelps, capturing the attention of Red, who drags Jimmy out of his office with a gun to his back. "Damn! Damn!" is all Red could say, watching his henchman and Digger both dead on the wooden floor. "You no good….come here!" Red threatens with his gun, motioning for Blue and Haynes to take a step towards him. Still holding the gun in his hand, Red shoves Jimmy to the side. He reaches out to Blue's throat, holding it in a tight grip. "You cost me my boys, but I'll take your lives!"

"No, stop!" Blue shouts in fear. Red clutches her throat to the point of crushing her larynx. Haynes couldn't let that happen. Her future – and theirs depends on it. Closing his eyes, he bolts toward Red, tackling him to the ground. They struggle, and two shots burst from Red's gun. One causes Haynes to scream in pain while the other forces Red to drop his gun on the ground. During the struggle, Red's gun discharges at an unfortunate target; the gun holder himself. Haynes's shoulder bled with an overflowing spot of red through his shirt. Jimmy calls for an ambulance and the police, who undoubtedly heard the gunshots from inside the club. Blue holds her throat, tears pouring from her eyes tending to her man on the floor, bleeding profusely. Haynes raises his eyes quietly, praying this wouldn't be his last minute on earth. He had unexpectedly achieved so much this past day and night; it would be a shame if he didn't enjoy all that he has gained. It would be a waste to see it all gone now.

Hearing a sound, Haynes slowly opens his eyelids, instantly closing at the bright array of light surrounding them. They flicker back and forth, adjusting to the white-colored walls of a room. His body lies motionless, resting on a bed. Blue lowers her hand, touching the side of his face, wiping it away. He sees Jimmy leaning against the wall, smoking a cigarette. He looks around for Deke. Slowly using his elbows to rise out of his bed, Blue urges him to lay back down. His right shoulder burns with pain, forcing him to lay back down. Jimmy approaches the bed shaking his head, standing next to Blue. "You need to take it easy. The doctors said you'll be out today if you just lay still."

The realization hits Haynes: he is in a hospital. Swerving his head left and right, questions form in his mind filtering down to his lips. "Where's Deke? Is he all right? Where is he?"

Blue lightly touches his cheek. Her skin glows accentuated by the light blue dress she wears. Jimmy shakes his head in remorse. "I'm afraid Deke's gone on to meet his mama in heaven." Hearing those words, Haynes's eyes begin to flood with tears. His heart grieves for his dead friend. "No, no!" He cries out. Blue comforts him. "Hey baby, it's all right. I'm here." Her voice sounds restricted, strained. Haynes suspects Red's grip did something to do with that. "How are you, songbird?"

"Not too well, to be honest. That bad man did something to my throat when he held it as tight as he did. The doctors said he crushed my larynx. They advised me to take it easy with my voice, but every time I try to sing, it sounds like this." Haynes hears Blue struggle to sing a note, not like last night, where her voice was flawless. Haynes and Jimmy look on as Blue slumps downward, defeated. She knew the possibility of never regaining what she had lost. Her hopes and dreams shattered in an instant.

Somehow, she retrieves the strength to turn back to Haynes and place a gentle hand on his cheek. "I don't…. I don't want to think about it anymore. I'm just glad you're all right."

"Hey, songbird. You'll always sound good to me. I…. I love you." Overcome by emotion, Haynes declares his feelings for her. Blue responds with joyful tears, leaning down to give a warm embrace to Haynes. Jimmy nods in approval. Tender kisses were exchanged between the lovers, happy they have lived through an ordeal that could have ended much differently. Jimmy steps back in front of the bed after allowing the lovers to have their moment by stepping away.

"I just want to share this with you two; last night before trouble went down was perfect. We couldn't ask for a better crowd, and before those men burst into my office, we did well for one night. I wish we could have more nights like that, but Blue's condition and surviving our robbery attempt made me come up with this decision along with the family's; we're going to shut down the club."

Blue and Haynes stare at Jimmy with surprised looks on their faces. "Jimmy, no! My voice may not be the best, but I'll be all right." Blue pleads with Jimmy shaking his head.

"Blue, the doctors told me in the hallway just now that ruffian severely damaged your larynx. You just showed Haynes and me that it wouldn't be a good idea to have you sing tonight. Deke and Digger are dead. What use is it to reopen a club when that's all patrons will talk about? The family agrees with the decision. Club Sullivan is no more."

Haynes shakes his head, refusing to believe Jimmy's decision. Disgruntled, he lies back down on the bed, watching Blue lower herself to wrap her arms around him for a hug. "It'll be all right, baby. We still have each other. I love you."

Accepting the inevitable, Haynes responds. "I love you too. It doesn't matter what happens; we have each other. No one or nothing will take us……. wait! Stop!" Watching Blue stand up, Haynes is helpless to act watching her as she is engulfed in a great white light. Jimmy also fades within the mysterious light flooding the room and all within its walls. Stretching out a hand, Haynes cries out Blue's name as she fades within the light. The last image he sees from her is her smiling face towards him. She is overtaken by the light, fading away into nothingness; Jimmy and the room were next to vanish. There was nothing Haynes could do.

Before Haynes could react, he faces another bright shining light in his eyes. The light is from the flashlight of a young Latina uniformed police officer who stands above him. She is accompanied by a taller, slimmer Caucasian officer, also in uniform. Their faces reflect calmness yet ready to anticipate trouble. Haynes's reaction proves to them he's not a threat.

"Hey, hey, mister!" The female officer yells softly at Haynes, poking at him. He begins to stir into consciousness, feeling the pull of the male officer pulling him up out of the debris on the dirt-laden floor. "Are you all right?" She asks. Her facial features are youthful, attractive. Her voice is direct but not aggressive. "You shouldn't be here. Do you have a home?"

"Where am I?" Haynes asks, disoriented and glassy eyed with the realization he has returned to a place he did not desire to be. "Where's Blue? I wanted to tell her that I love her."

The female officer glances at her muscular partner. He shrugs his broad shoulders displaying a confused face. "Maybe we should take him to the new shelter on Adams?"

"Mister, do you have a home? Do you live in a shelter?" The female officer questions Haynes, who looks around the deserted club. There was nothing recognizable that he could see. The lounge, the stage, and the bar were gone. In their places were dusty and worn wooden tables, chairs, and an unrecognizable area that could have been named Club Sullivan, but it wasn't. "Where is it?" Haynes asks the female officer. "What happened to it? Where's the club?"

"What are you talking about?" Her face contorts to a puzzled look. Her male counterpart parts his lips to answer. "I heard this from one of the guys. Before it turned into a Mexican restaurant, this place used to be a nightclub a long time ago. They told me their grandparents used to go here and the Dunbar hotel. They said it closed down a long time ago, left vacant for a few years before a family moved in and turned the place into that restaurant."

"Where is she?" Haynes shouts. "What happened to Blue? I need to see her!"

"Hey, hey, mister. Tell you what we're going to do." The female officer holds up a hand. "Instead of arresting you for trespassing, we're going to drive you to a shelter on Adams Boulevard. We know the manager, so she will take care of you."

"She's good with new attendees. At least you'll have a decent place to stay tonight." The male officer replies.

Haynes nods his head reluctantly, believing he could never return to that night in the world of Club Sullivan. He gained so much there; friends, a good job, and a woman who will be forever lost in his mind. The officers lead him to the squad car outside.

The vacant space of the former Club Sullivan before its conversion now lies quietly in shadow. There were no sounds of local jazz bands playing on stage, the voices of talented singers, not even a festive atmosphere of patrons frequenting the club to enjoy evenings of lively entertainment. Yet, somewhere within this space, there is a voice. A voice filled with the melodic verse with the color blue. Scattered by debris and left empty within the walls of this former club filled with Black faces is a place that forever will be lost in the tides of time. Club Sullivan closed its doors for the last time that night as many such clubs and establishments on Central Avenue in South Los Angeles. Only the fading sounds of a storied past remain. A history waiting for its rightful place to return.

What Is Truth?

Centuries ago
Pilate
Roman procurator
asked Jesus The Christ
Son of the Creator
a question
which today puzzles Man
we find it difficult
hard to understand
should we be courageous
committed to the root
we'll find the answer to
"What is truth?"

What is truth
that lasts beyond time?
Where can it be found
to elevate our minds?
How do we apply it
to inspire our generation
heal our many wounds
uplift our nation?
Wordsworth
remarkable sage
defined it poetically, scripting on page
"truth is more than truth."
a desire, a creed

in this dire time
a drug we surely need
"of zeal by authority Divine
sanctioned, of danger
difficulty or death."
shouldn't this be
Mankind's greatest quest
instead of chasing
unpromised treasured wealth?

The task is set ahead of thee
do we settle for
the summer of illusion
or the harsh winter of reality?
growing up we have witnessed
justice prevail
unfortunately
so have lies
truth is like a light
for those who seek to hide it
urges a quiet demise
but let us be like Pilate
ask what is truth
then seek to find an answer
in the hope together
may we rid ourselves
of Man's deceitful cancer.

I Got Some News For Ya

This is Brother Truth
on the mic
expressing thoughts
you might not like
addressing all within
the Dark nation
coming to you live
from an underground station.

You say I'm a hater, that's right
I hate ignorance
whether it's day or night
I tell you this admission
right up in your face
I despise
the mental cancer eating away
at the core of our proud race.

Who the blank I think I am
you shout my way
wondering out loud
I'm a conscious soldier
Black and proud
with thoughts
that live inside of me
daring to say
what's on my mind
taking a stand being brave

saying my my my
a green piece of paper
from the White man
may set us free
but within our race
we're still enslaved
I hope you agree.

Young sisters
stop spreading your legs
like peanut butter
unless you ready
for the responsibility
of being a mother
young soldier
pull up your pants and pride
shock the world
with what God
has blessed you inside.

You ask
why am I raising all this fuss?
because ignorance
is taking away the very best of us
putting limits on self
chaining each other
or so it seems
bowing down to reality
giving up our dreams.

If we had this attitude
a century prior
we would never have
DeBois, Washington
Malcolm, King, Douglass
men of color
setting our sights higher
instead of smoking weed
these men stood up
not hanging with their boys
saying 'I don't give a -.'

Positivity is what I stress
but now it's about time
to put away this
wasteful foolishness
drinking dirty liquor
sipping on the demon
like you just don't care
you know deep in your heart
you'll never find that poison
on the Westside or Bel Air
smokin and puffin
from herbs that grow
straight from the ground
young brothers and sisters
you do know that apple
Adam and Eve bit
It wasn't cool too
they got run

out of Paradise's town.

So I say to these young people
hear me and hear me now
just don't think my words
won't come true presently
if not, then the future somehow.

Examine your lives
reach for the heights
aim to be greater
then you too shall know what it's like
to be an ignorance hater.
Peace Out.

Forever

Forever
its meaning for a limitless time
that's how long I thought
you would be mine
the woman who healed my heart
committed to a meaningful relationship
we made that vow to hold fast that word
spoken from our lips.

However
one cannot accurately forecast
the future
though we learn from the past
to judge only the present
no longer are we as one
truth so evident
I remember a while ago
we planned a loving, peaceful fate
unaware of the reality the two of us
would break up as mates.

Cold nights
the sullen emptiness of a bed
finding motivation
to keep you going in your head
glaring at CD's
playing songs of love
romantic daydreams

all a void now listening to tunes
meant for lonely hearts
fill up my time every day, it seems.
Emotions used up
sitting on a floor adjusting to reflect
all the positive moments
we shared very close to perfect
I'll love you always
hoping you feel equal as my heart
you'll always be special
but we must live
our lives apart.

Forever.
Reader, please
choose those words carefully
to the one you love
though your feelings swell
to celestial Heaven above
time will prove whether your vow
is truly meant
for your loved one
it is my sincerest hope
to you and your mate ring true
from sunrise
to the setting of the romantic sun.

The Drug of Racism

Here in America, we have a number of addictions
Throw in drugs, greed, and include racism
Prejudice is a drug dangerously
sweeping the nation
Serious as a world threat or superpower invasion.

Blacks mistrusting whites,
whites mistrusting blacks
Sources of respect are evil hearts lack
Other cultures and races tossed in the hate game
Freebasing on hate, burning up in flames.

History records uncover this substance abuse
Morals were misguided and social codes lose
Armies slaughtered races, creations of God
The dead pay the price for the blood they trod.

Little children aren't affected; they're colorblind
For they are pure in heart, cleansed in the mind
Only when society bombards them in condition
They accept and absorb its racist traditions.

If this is America and her states are united
Then why are its citizens painfully divided?
To stop racist addictions, there must be a start
To ban this drug and purify many hearts.

We Are Born Alone

We are born into
this world alone
from beginning to end
this is the life
I own.

No one else can take my place
even if someone
happens to share the same face.

There is no one
whose heart pumps
takes breaths
within my shell
either my destination
at life's end shall be
the gates of heaven
or torment
at the fires of hell.

Therefore I live
my individual life as best I can
whatever awaits me
at the finish
I will face it
like a man.

Where I Live

Little boys
on a front porch
playing Digit Digit
Number Nine
girls across the street
doing the Double Dutch
trying to stay within the lines
an elderly man waters his lawn
before it turns dark
young men hooping
some pickup games
at a local park.

This was typical
in the neighborhood
I lived in when my age was singular
growing up on the Southside
before bullets flew
turning sidewalks
into a flowing red tide
years before Nine Eleven
we were the ones
watching our backs
lest the person
behind you had a gun
two colored rags
shook quiet serenity
put our area on the map

creating an unfortunate identity.

All we had in the hood
was each other
because it was common
to hear the news
a pistol smoked another brother
citizens cried out long before
'protect us from crime.'
not surprisingly
they went unheeded
over time
so you have to understand
folks a tad bit resentful
when our concerns
were finally addressed
finally in the know
during a civil revolt
resulting from an unjust verdict
drama made for media shows.

Speaking of the media
from small stations
to giants like Fox
why is it in prime time
we don't show more pictures
of college graduates
holding diplomas in hand
instead of gold-plated glocks?

oh well, I just thought
I throw out that question
it seems our young folks
need an alternative
examples of positivity
would be
a profitable direction.

But to those living in South L.A.
and areas nearby
bad-mouthed by hosts of radio talk
we agree the Coliseum
and the old Sports Arena
are the only places they walk
to those I've seen, spoken to
laughed, cried with
and even patted my back
I'm proud to have met each one of you
telling me to stay on track
though times are different
the world around us
turns ignorant and cold
you continue to stand strong
show that Southside pride
as we walk together, bold.